———————— ★ ————————

"OFFICER DOWN!"

Someone was choking, someone was sobbing, and he hoped it wasn't him, but he had a terrible feeling it was because he couldn't see Tos very well now. The big man was just lying there, with the blood pouring down his face and dripping off his nose and chin—already there was a big puddle on the floor. He pressed the button on the handset again.

"Code 9—officer down," he whispered. "Please..."

———————— ★ ————————

"Gosling knows how to delicately tie up readers' nerve endings."

—*Booklist*

Also available from Worldwide Mystery by
PAULA GOSLING

THE WYCHFORD MURDERS
MONKEY PUZZLE

BACKLASH

PAULA GOSLING

W🌐RLDWIDE.

TORONTO • NEW YORK • LONDON • PARIS
AMSTERDAM • STOCKHOLM • HAMBURG
ATHENS • MILAN • TOKYO • SYDNEY

BACKLASH

A Worldwide Mystery/October 1991

Published by agreement with Doubleday, a division of
Bantam Doubleday Dell Publishing Group, Inc.

ISBN 0-373-26082-2

BACKLASH

THE GUN LAY on a white cloth below the window, its parts dismantled, ready for cleaning.

The killer stood beside it, waiting for the day.

In the dark streets below, traffic lights blinked red, yellow, and green over empty intersections. No cars passed. Department store windows glared their wares at one another across the long, silent avenues. A newspaper skittered by in the gutter, caught by a sudden, secret breeze.

Somewhere in the park, a bird sang.

The day was coming.

Gradually, the rising light revealed the surrounding buildings, standing like a silent crowd of alien, angular beings. Hundreds of blank windows reflected stratified clouds riding high over the horizon, their undersides incandescent. The snaking curves of the river that cut the city in two slowly turned to old mercury, hazed and dully gleaming.

Suddenly, from the far side of the city, a jumbo jet knifed upwards, seemed to hang motionless for a moment, then turned away in a long, graceful curve, trailing a spider's thread of white vapour that caught fire from the rising sun.

Now the light was stronger, brighter, filling the apartment. It glowed back from the polished surfaces of the furniture, the rich colours of the upholstery, the glass in the photograph frames, the silver trophies on the mantelpiece, the other guns in the wall rack, and the empty circle of the mirror above the carved mahogany desk.

The killer went to the mirror and gazed into it.

The face within was bland, unremarkable.

That was what made it special.

Nobody knew, nobody even guessed.

One dead last night.

Maybe another tomorrow.

The killer smiled.

Mirror, mirror on the wall—

Who's the cleverest one of all?

ONE

STRYKER WATCHED THE PLANE lift from the runway, so big, so heavy, that it seemed impossible it could break from the earth and soar free. But soar it did, until it became a small dot curving away into the sky. For a moment there was a glint, a spark of sunlight from it, and then it became dull, dark grey, and—nothing.

Gradually he became aware of the airport around him—shops, ticket counters, seats for the weary and the waiting, restaurants, snack bars, and the constant flow of human beings from place to place, restless with the sense of travel that permeated every corner of the vast building.

"Heraclitus," he muttered.

"Go on," Tos said, beside him, in that flat tell-me-another voice he had begun using lately whenever Stryker spoke some impenetrable and pseudo-academic piece of rubbish. "Him? Never."

Stryker looked up and grinned. "Said the world and everything in it was in a constant state of flux, changing and flowing."

"No kidding. What with going bald, changing my underwear every day, and having to cut the lawn regularly, I never noticed. Is there a cure or do we just have to put up with it?"

"He didn't say."

"That's the thing about those old Greeks," Tos said. "All questions and no answers."

"A bit like police work?"

"I was just going to say that."

Stryker nodded. "I thought you were." They moved away from the observation windows and started across the concourse, dodging the darting children, the occasional suitcase corner, and the uninformed flunkies with clipboards who scuttled from one place to another to relay more very vital statistics.

Halfway across they met Pinsky coming the other way.

"What the hell are you doing here?" Tos asked. Pinsky looked grim, and was sweating slightly, as if he had been running.

"Kate get off all right?" he asked Stryker.

"I'm afraid so—despite an impassioned last-minute plea," Stryker said.

"Mostly about dirty shirts and how to load the dishwasher," Tos put in. "It was very moving."

"Moving is what I came to get you about. We've got another one." The other two waited. "Plainclothes, this time," Pinsky went on quietly. "In the parking lot outside his own precinct house."

"Like the others?" Tos asked.

Pinsky nodded. "Like the others. In the head."

IT HAD STARTED about ten days before.

First victim, a cop named Richard Santosa, shot in the head while investigating a prowler report in a perfectly respectable neighbourhood. His own precinct detectives began investigating the case, following up Santosa's private life, looking into recent arrest involvements, anything that might give them a reason for his murder. This was the reasonable pursuit of routine.

The second victim, Merrilee Trask, was shot while calling in an abandoned car license number. Different precinct, opposite side of town, and *their* detectives began to pursue the same routine and prescribed course as their colleagues were following in the Santosa murder.

Until Ballistics paired the bullets.

The two precincts liaised, gingerly at first, coordinating their investigations and pooling information. What was the link between Santosa, a good-looking bachelor, and Trask, a divorced woman? The obvious connection—that they had been seeing one another off the job—was quickly discounted. Santosa had a steady girlfriend, and the two victims had never met.

And then the killer hit again. Third victim, Sandy Randolph, was shot while returning from investigating an arson report. His partner had been hurt when their car went off the road and hit a telephone pole, and so had not been able to pursue the killer, who had fired from a passing car.

Randolph was nearly thirty, black, had been married a year, and was about to leave the uniformed branch and train in computers with an eye to either working with them or teaching trainee cops to do so. He liked police theory, but not street work.

Yet another precinct, yet another professional "family" involved. Although this killing had been done with a handgun—the first two had been rifles—there was a general agreement that the three might be connected. They all seemed to be motiveless murders, all were head shots, all cops.

The case was turned over to Central Homicide.

The task that faced them was monumental. That there was a common killer seemed probable. But was he killing at random, or was there a deeper reason behind the murders?

If it was random, there was nothing to be done but increase their vigilance, follow up all the tips and rumours that came in, check out gun shops for new or unusual sales of weapons or ammunition, go over files of known cop haters and other assorted psychos.

And wonder about all the others that weren't on the files.

If, on the other hand, there was some motivating factor, some pattern to the killings, what was it and where could they find it? Where could they *begin* to find it? All they had to work with were the victims themselves. They put the computer to work, looking for an answer. It came up with thousands of possibilities. Each one had to be followed up. There were only so many officers in the department. As many as could be spared were put to work checking out the leads the computer threw out.

Leaving the rest to keep up with the day-to-day work that faced them whether they were being shot at or not. Of course, in the interest of public safety and private anguish, they would have liked to keep all this activity to themselves.

Unfortunately for the department, police reporters are not deaf and they are certainly not dumb. The minute the papers put it together and began screaming cop killer, the already over-stretched departmental ranks began to waver and wane.

Randolph's partner, Frank Richmond, had been severely shocked by having his partner's head blown apart while they were driving quietly down the street, and had quit the force shortly after leaving hospital.

He was not the first.

Those in the department who had been uncertain of their vocation suddenly became terribly interested in selling real estate, taking up plumbing, going back to school to study law, agriculture, or applied art. Even old hands, good hands, found themselves whistling in the dark, looking over their shoulders, and watching the high places.

Those civilians who had been toying with the idea of joining the police decided maybe something else, such as skydiving or professional football, would be the safer alternative.

The reason for the growing panic was simple, and had little to do with closing ranks or seeking revenge. It had to do with simple logic.

A person who would kill a cop respects no one.
A person who would kill a cop would kill anyone.

Anyone.

TWO

THE PARKING LOT was gritty asphalt, surrounded by high walls, and overlooked by buildings on all four sides. Fat clouds in the sky overhead cast occasional shadows, so the scene continually flickered from bright sunlight to momentary dusk, and back again. Police cars, both marked and unmarked, were herringboned into the limited space. Added to them now was a constantly shifting population of onlookers, both uniformed and plainclothes. In the alternating brightness there was a constant putting on and taking off of sunglasses. Nobody wanted to miss a thing.

The centre of activity was at the far corner of the lot—a figure in sports coat and flannels, face down between a Chevy station wagon and the high wall, what was left of his head surrounded by a halo of blood, brain matter, and bone fragments. Beside him crouched Bannerman, the medical examiner. It was fortunate he was so tall and bony, otherwise it would have been difficult for him to get near the body. As it was he had to stand up fairly frequently to avoid a cramp. Every time he did, the other members of the team would start to get out of his way, thinking he was finished, only to filter back when he crouched down again.

Stryker squinted up at the surrounding offices and apartment buildings. This was not a rich precinct, neither was it a slum. As the cancer of inner-city rot spread wider and wider, so it would engulf this area as it had many others. Already he could see blank windows of empty offices, and the occasional torn curtain of an abandoned apartment. There were loungers on the street corners, now and again a drunk slept in a doorway. It was coming, but it wasn't here. "These buildings been checked out?" he asked.

Captain Corsa looked at him, his black eyes glinting over his fat olive cheeks, like animals watching from cover. "What do you think?"

"Sorry," Stryker said.

Corsa scowled. "He must have been lying there most of the night; nobody noticed him until the dawn shift came on." Corsa rubbed his face and pinched his nose and sighed. "We had a beer over at Whistles when we came off shift last night. We did that sometimes. Then he said he had to get home, he'd been sleeping bad and wanted to get his head down." Corsa paused, swallowed, continued in a flat voice. "He has a wife and three small kids. He was a decent cop—about to take his lieutenant's exams. Also a friend."

"Sorry," Stryker said, again.

Corsa nodded. "Yeah, aren't we all? He's the fourth, isn't he? Fourth or fifth?"

"Fourth," Tos said.

"It stinks," Corsa said, turning away and staring at the tops of the buildings opposite. "What have you got on this?"

"We have four dead cops in four separate precincts," Stryker said grimly. "Three uniformed and now Yentall, here, in plainclothes. The first three never served together. They were all different ranks, different ages, different descriptions, different everything. Yentall might make a match with one or all of them. Maybe he won't. So far, it makes no sense."

"Same gun?"

Tos shook his head. "First two, rifle. Next one, handgun, probably a .38, although the bullet fragmented so they aren't certain. What they have in common is that they're all cops, they were all shot in the head, and nobody can figure out the motive. Maybe this one is different—maybe he had gotten threats, or had a known enemy, whatever. We'll go into that with you. That's all we've got. One thing— the first two were picked off from over five hundred yards, the other from a moving car."

"Marksman," Corsa observed.

"A lot of them around," Stryker said. "These days."

This time, when Bannerman stood up, he was finished. He edged out from between the car and the wall and came towards Stryker and the others. "This one was different. Done from close up," he said.

"Same gun as before?"

Bannerman shrugged. "Not my department, but I'd be surprised if they could tell anything except the calibre. Definitely a handgun. It went through him and hit the wall—a lump of lead is all there is. Maybe a .38." He hefted the little grey lump in its labelled plastic bag, then put it in his pocket. "You want to look before we take him away?"

"No thanks," Tos said, going a little pale.

Bannerman looked at him and half smiled. "You've got to get over that sometime, Tos, if you want to get a promotion."

"I'll stick," Tos said. "Thanks just the same."

Stryker sighed. "I'll go."

It was not an edifying sight, and he took in as much as he could as fast as he could. Maybe Toscarelli's weak stomach was catching. Or maybe it was just anger that wrenched at his stomach when he looked down on a fellow officer who had been slaughtered for no apparent reason. One of the photographers took another shot, and the flash rebounded off the wedding band on the victim's left hand.

Stryker glanced up at the sky and thought of Kate, by now high above the ocean, going to England for a literary conference. He hadn't said much to her about the first three cop killings, but she read the papers like everyone else. She hadn't said anything about them either—she didn't have to. It lay between them, as it had from the beginning—every time he went out the door it could be for the last time, and she didn't want to bring kids up on her own. He always tried to point out that a plainclothes officer was far less likely to get killed than a uniformed one—but what would he have told her if she'd been waiting at home for him tonight? Detective Phil Yentall lay at his feet, tweed jacket, grey flannel slacks, pale blue shirt, no tie, no uniform. Casual as they come.

Mrs. Yentall would be bringing up three kids alone.

He went back to Corsa and Tos with less than the usual spring in his step. "Bastard," was all he said.

He didn't mean Yentall.

PARTNERS ARE FUNNY THINGS.

Especially when they're cops. If you're a cop you don't have to like your partner (although it helps), but you sure as hell have to trust him or her. You have to *know*.

Lieutenant Jack Stryker and Sergeant "Tos" Toscarelli had been partners for some years. It was not a formal or permanent assignment—police partnerships never are. But it is a foolish captain of police who does not quickly realise which men work well together, and their particular captain—although he had his failings—was not a foolish man. Even when Stryker moved up to lieutenant, the relationship between Toscarelli and himself had remained firm and productive.

Some people wondered how Stryker put up with Toscarelli's affectionate bullying—they said Tos was a classic case of "Jewish mother," despite the fact that he was a devout Catholic and attended Mass regularly. Stryker's hair was curly, receding, and had recently gone prematurely white. He claimed this was a result of the traumatic experience of falling in love, but it was a family trait. It gave him a specious appearance of maturity. The fact was, he needed a mother and he knew it. He moved fast and his mind moved fast—sometimes so fast it went right by things like raincoats, meals, and sleep. He didn't like to clutter up his brain with himself.

He loved and lived with Kate Trevorne, a professor of English at the university. At home they shared the chores of living as some couples do—she did most of the work and he appreciated it. But it was still left to Tos to make sure Stryker didn't fall into rivers or miss too many meals while on a case. What would happen when Toscarelli eventually married and had kids of his own only time would tell.

There was a serious risk that Stryker might have to grow up.

Then there was the partnership of Neilson and Pinsky.

When Detective Harvey Neilson had first been transferred to plainclothes at Central Homicide and had been partnered with Sergeant Ned Pinsky, he'd figured the thing would last maybe four or five days. Neilson was young, athletic, single, good-looking, quick-witted, and extremely attractive to women—a blessing he took no trouble to disguise. As far as he could see, Pinsky was slow-thinking, slow-talking, and a real hick. Of course, everybody *liked* Pinsky, but Neilson figured this was because Pinsky was no threat to anyone and apparently always good for a contribution to somebody's birthday present collection. Neilson figured he'd look so good next to a loser like Pinsky that his natural ability would soon be rewarded, and he would quickly be promoted to chief of police by a grateful commissioner.

It hadn't happened yet.

At first Harvey found his lack of recognition pretty galling. After all, he'd come tops in all his exams from day one, had been fast and tough in uniform, and had been transferred to plainclothes quickly because he and everyone else knew he'd be a terrific detective, right? Whereas Pinsky, on the other hand, must have gotten to Central Homicide by some kind of bureaucratic mess-up, or he was somebody's brother-in-law. Had to be *something* like that.

But when old Pinsky kept getting the answers before Quicksilver Harvey the Shining Hope of Homicide, it began to be apparent even to Neilson that there must be more to the hick than first met the eye. True, Pinsky looked as if he had been put together with string and sealing wax by a blind one-armed puppet maker, but he gangled along pretty smartly when it was necessary.

In fact, he'd had to move very fast in order to save Neilson's life, about a year back. They had been called to the scene of a robbery with violence, arriving within a minute of the call, as they had been only a street away. The owner of the liquor shop was lying dead in his own doorway, and the killer was rifling the cash register as they pulled up. He fled out the back door and they followed. Within another minute, the killer had put a slug into Neilson, but five seconds later had gone down himself with Pinsky's snap shot in his heart. Ned checked that the perpetrator was dead, called in, then gave Neilson first aid until the ambulance got there.

"How did you know the bastard was waiting back there?" Neilson had gasped as he lay in the alley trying hard not to bleed to death.

"Rat," Pinsky said.

"I agree, but how did you know he was there?"

"I saw a rat running away," Pinsky said patiently. "Also he was casting a shadow."

"The rat was casting a shadow?" Neilson's head was swimming.

"No—the guy that shot you was casting a shadow."

"I—ouch—never saw a shadow," Neilson objected. "I was looking."

"You didn't look up," Pinsky said. "The lights were on in the basement disco, right? With lights below, you get shadow above. In his case, on the bottom of a fire escape."

"Elementary, my dear Watson," Neilson muttered.

"He never said that, you know," Pinsky said conversationally, as he pressed his handkerchief down hard over Neilson's wound, watched his eyes and the pulse in his temple, and listened for the sirens. "Never *exactly* that, anyway. The closest he ever came was simply 'Elementary,' in 'The Crooked Man.' ''

"No kidding," Neilson said, and passed out.

In the following months, Neilson gradually began to understand about Pinsky. Pinsky was not a boy genius, or a master of insight, or a hot shot anything—Pinsky was the Practical Common Man. Pinsky was a pipe smoker. He read a lot. He went skiing in the winter, sailing in the summer. He had a big family—an adoring wife, decent kids, a dog that did tricks. He believed in justice. A psychiatrist would have said he was a well-integrated personality.

As Neilson was still trying to thrash out why life was always sneaking up on him, he came to find Pinsky's calm in the face of adversity a source of strength. Waiting for Pinsky to come up with something gave him time to clear his own head. This was exactly what Stryker had hoped would happen when he suggested pairing the two of them. "When they're together it will be common sense illuminated by flashes of lightning," he had told Captain Klotzman. "Trust me— they'll mesh." And they had.

These four, along with the assistance of other detectives as available, had been assigned to head the hunt for the cop killer. All leads, tips, suspicions, and rumours went to them, filtering up from the thousands of officers covering the city. Copies of all the paperwork went to them. Crank calls and voluntary "confessions" went to them. Complaints went to them. Questions from the press, from the public, from other officers went to them. The pressure came up from below and down from above, and in from outside.

And with each new death, the pressure increased.

Stryker and Tos went into the precinct station to continue their conversation with Captain Corsa and to check out Yentall's reports and assignments over the past few weeks. Neilson and Pinsky stayed in the courtyard. As they watched the coroner's men take away what was left of Detective Yentall, Pinsky was reflective, going over it again, going over it as they had gone over it every hour, every day, since it had landed in their laps.

"If it's random, we're stalled, right?"

"Oh right," Neilson said, furiously taking down notes of the scene.

"So let's assume it isn't random."

"I'm open to offers," Neilson muttered.

Pinsky gazed at the photographers packing up their equipment. "We started with long shots—now we've got a close-up."

"You what?" Neilson asked, still writing.

"Maybe three strangers, one friend."

Neilson's pen stopped and he looked up. "Some friend."

"Acquaintance, then," Pinsky conceded.

"Okay, it's a way in. But it could be the reverse—three from a distance because he might be recognised, one close up because the guy didn't know him from Adam," Neilson said. He closed his notebook. "I think we'd better start this one by talking to Yentall's partner—what was his name?"

"Sobell," Pinsky said. "I know him—he's a good man. He'll be pretty broken up about this."

Neilson looked at him with some curiosity. "Would you be broken up if I got blown away?" he asked.

Pinsky looked at him and thought about it. "I suppose it might get me down for a minute or two," he finally conceded.

Neilson raised an eyebrow. "As long as that?"

"Would you go into mourning for me?" Pinsky asked in turn.

"I would wear black for a year," Neilson said firmly.

"Yeah, well—you look good in black."

Neilson grinned. "I know." He closed his notebook. "Shall we adjourn to the drawing room and see what the rest of the party are doing? Then we can start running background comparisons with the others and see if the computer comes up with anything. I'd be grateful to find out if they all chewed the same kind of bubble gum when they were kids. I'm telling you, Ned, this thing is getting me down. I keep feeling this hot spot on the back of my head, as if it was a bright shiny target waiting to be hit."

Pinsky nodded. "As Sherlock Holmes would say— it's a bitch," he murmured as he shambled after Neilson.

THREE

SOBELL WAS A BALDING MAN with a fat moustache over a thin mouth. He was sitting at his desk, staring blankly at his torn blotter and ancient typewriter. He looked up when Pinsky and Neilson approached. For a fleeting moment, the sight of Ned Pinsky lit his brooding features, and then he relapsed into his former state.

"Harry," Ned said. "How're you doing?" He sat on the edge of Sobell's desk.

Sobell looked up. "I found him, Ned. I saw his car, I went over, and I found him. I recognised his jacket. His *jacket* for Chrissakes, not him. I thought I knew what it was like, losing somebody. We see it every day, don't we? But not this. This I can't handle. I'm sitting here, I'm dead inside, I don't know where each breath is coming from, I don't know how they keep coming, you know? Each one, I think, last time. I stop. And then I breathe again. Nothing to do with me, it just goes on and on and on—"

"Take it easy, Harry," Pinsky said.

"He was a good man," Sobell said. "We all say that, all the time when somebody dies, but Phil *was* a good man. A sweet man, you know? Everybody liked Phil. I loved him like a brother, we worked together maybe ten years, and I only recognised his damn *jacket*." Sobell was crying now.

"Had he said anything lately?" Neilson asked. "Like, anything about the sniper or anything?"

Sobell shook his head. "Nothing the rest of us weren't saying, like why don't we get the bastard and so on." He looked at Neilson. "Why don't we?"

Neilson sighed. "We're trying. You know how it is, you know how hard it is—"

"I know Phil is dead today," Sobell said flatly. "I know the first guy got it weeks ago."

"Yeah, but it was only last week somebody decided to put it together and drop it on us downtown," Pinsky said. "It's like climbing a mountain, Harry—stuff keeps sliding down into your face. We keep looking for connections, we keep hoping for a pattern."

Sobell's face twisted. "Then lucky you—here's another guy down to add to your goddamn pattern."

"I didn't mean that," Pinsky said.

Sobell slumped in his chair and rubbed his face, wiping away the tears with the flat of his hands. "I know you didn't. I know the job. I can imagine what you're up against. But Jesus, Ned—why Phil?"

Pinsky looked around the room. Normally, like any precinct house at mid-morning, it would be crowded with people shouting and arguing and hectic with activity. Now it was unnaturally quiet, and what business there was was being conducted in low tones. This was a house of mourning. One of their own was gone. Every phone that rang seemed to jerk a knife through the atmosphere. The uniformed and plainclothes officers moving about their work were grim-faced and tense.

Pinsky looked at Sobell. "Why any of them?" he asked.

"THE OBVIOUS THING is somebody with a grudge," Stryker told Captain Corsa. "We're concentrating most of our efforts on old convictions at the moment. Looking for somebody they all put away who's been maybe building up a grudge while in prison. Somebody recently out would be first choice. Following that, we're working backwards through those not so recently out and so on. It's a hell of a job, I'm telling you."

"Which one isn't?" Corsa said, staring out of his window at the street in front of the precinct station. It was filling up with the curious and the morbid, who were drawn by the increased activity around the building—ambulance, medical examiner's car, cars belonging to the forensic team, the investigating team of detectives, and the uniformed officers searching the area for clues. This latter activity was largely pointless as any possible clue would have been long since obliterated by the crowds, the cars, the ambulance, et cetera, et cetera, et cetera.

But it had to be done.

"It all has to be done," Stryker said. "It's bad enough when you've got one scene of crime, one death, but *four*—four scenes, four sets of forensics, four backgrounds, four separate investigations intersecting with one another and one overall investigation—" He ran his hands through his hair in exasperation. "And all this time the bastard is out there, laughing at us."

Corsa turned to look at him. "You feel that? You feel one guy?"

"You bet your ass I do," Stryker said.

"What does he feel like?" Corsa asked.

Stryker sighed and began to walk around the room. As it was small and crowded with furniture and filing cabinets, his passage was neither easy nor straightforward. Corsa's question was not a facetious one, especially not to Stryker. Most detectives investigating a crime—particularly homicide—get a sense of their quarry. Whether it comes through eyes and ears or past experiences or instinct or something unqualified and unnamed, it nevertheless comes.

"Cold," Stryker said. "He feels like a cold bastard to me. Not hot, not crazy. Careful, deliberate. Implacable."

"Man with a mission? Sounds like you're describing a soldier, maybe. Someone like that."

Stryker nodded. "Maybe. An executioner. That's what he feels like."

"Professional hit man?" Corsa asked.

Stryker raised his shoulders high, then let them fall. "Maybe. We haven't gotten that far, yet, we're still up to our asses in local psychos and old grudges, like I said. If somebody is paying him to do this, we're into a whole new line of country. Could be somebody with a reason to hate or fear these particular victims, or a campaign against the whole department, in which case we're probably back to random targets again."

"Christ—there's too much to get hold of there." Corsa was sympathetic. Being a local precinct captain, the scope of Stryker's investigation hadn't really hit him yet. He dealt with the day-to-day problems of his men and his area. Even now, when one of his own was part of it, he was shaken by the task Stryker had been set. "What if it's political? What if it's some fanatical group—"

Stryker smiled, and nodded. "Now you're getting the idea. What if it's a program against the whole of society? That's supposed to be the recommended pattern, isn't it, to destabilize the established order? Good place to start, killing off the police and scaring the shit out of them so they can't function efficiently. Because we aren't functioning efficiently, city-wide, at the moment. You can't do a decent job if you're always looking over your shoulder. So, what if it's the beginning of a goddamn revolution? Where do I look for the bastard then? Hey? Nobody has come forward to say 'This is down to us,' but maybe they're just waiting for the best opportunity. Or maybe they want to take out a few more before they hit the headlines. And every time they kill, the problem gets bigger, the possibilities get more numerous, and the work expands to fill and overflow the available hours and men. Got any suggestions, Captain?"

"Tranquilizers," Corsa said. "You're wearing a hole in my carpet already."

Stryker smiled bleakly. "Sorry—I always do this when I'm thinking."

Corsa nodded, then tilted his head back, as if listening. "Maybe you should sit down and take a few deep breaths. It's going to get worse any minute now."

"What makes you say that?"

Corsa directed his thumb over his shoulder towards the window. "Can't you hear the baying of the hounds? The press have arrived."

"JESUS, I HATE THIS," Stryker said, standing just inside the entrance.

"Let Neilson do it; he's prettier than you," Tos suggested.

"No thanks," Neilson said.

"Don't look at me." Pinsky put his hands up, as if to ward off Toscarelli's eyes. "I freeze up when Nell gets out the kids' camera."

"Besides," Neilson pointed out. "You've done it before. You're used to it."

"You never get used to it," Stryker snapped, looking down to see if his fly was zipped and his tie was straight. "Jesus, I hate this."

They went out through the precinct doors and stood on the top step. Immediately a volley of flashguns went off, temporarily blinding them and momentarily stopping their hearts.

They sounded like so many shots.

A bouquet of microphones blossomed under Stryker's chin as radio and television reporters surged forwards and broke through the ranks of their newsprint colleagues. The questions surged over them like the waves off Molokai.

"Who's the latest victim?"

"Is it true it's another woman?"

"Have you got the killer yet?"

"Why haven't you got the killer yet?"

"How many are dead now?"

"What are you doing to catch the killer?"

"What's the dead man's name?"

"Who is responsible for the investigation?"

"How do you spell your last name?"

"Do you think it's some kind of revenge thing?"

"Is it true they call you 'Jumping Jack?' "

"How was he killed?"

"Was he shot in the head like the rest?"

"Was he in uniform?"

"What's his name?"

"When was he killed?"

"Why was he killed?"

"Is it true he wasn't discovered until this morning?"

"Was it a rifle?"

"Was it a handgun?"

"Who's going to be the next victim?"

"Is it only cops—or is it anyone?"

"What are you going to do about it?"

The noise was deafening, one question overlapping another, each shout louder than the one preceding it. The crowd was jostling its way up the stairs, like some amoebic monster with many heads and feet and hands. Dotted here and there were the blank glassy eyes of the hand-held television cameras, staring at him, closing in. Stryker stifled the impulse to turn and run. He took a deep breath. Now then.

He raised his hands and felt like a magician must feel when a trick works out. Everybody fell quiet, instantly. He raised his voice and spoke carefully.

"This morning a police officer was found dead, here in his precinct parking lot. He had been shot. We have no way of knowing at this time whether it is an isolated incident or part of a larger investigation. His name will be released this afternoon, when his family has been properly notified. It is true that a number of police officers have been killed—"

They couldn't stand it. First one voice interrupted, then another, then another.

"This makes four."

"All shot in the head."

"Was he shot in the head?"

"Who was he? What's his name?"

"Why don't you do something to protect the public?"

Stryker raised his voice above the returning flood of questions. "As far as we know the public are not at risk. It is your police who are at risk. We are accustomed to risks, that's our job. We are doing everything possible to catch the perpetrator—"

He was losing. He was sinking.

"What are you doing?"

"What steps are you taking?"

"What about the public?"

He could feel himself growing angry, felt the pressure building up in his skull. He knew his face was getting red, and he felt Toscarelli move up beside him on one side, Pinsky and Neilson on the other. For some reason, this seemed to amuse the reporters. The questions changed tone.

"Who are those guys?"

"Are they your bodyguards?"

"Are you going to put bodyguards on the police?"

"Are the police going into hiding?"

"Why haven't you called in the FBI?"

"Why don't you get Rambo?"

"Hey, maybe it *is* Rambo?"

"Why don't you catch this guy?"

"Why don't you stop him?"

At that moment the ambulance started up its siren and began to move slowly out of the entrance to the parking lot and through the crowd. The driver blew his horn at the vans and cars of the television stations which were blocking his way, and people began to surge towards the ambulance to get a look inside. The television people ran towards the cars of the forensic team who were emerging from the parking lot carrying their mysterious and ever-fascinating black cases. Only a few newspapermen remained behind with Stryker and the others.

One of them, an old hand named Ballinger, smiled wryly up at Stryker, who was wiping his face with his handkerchief.

"Anything we can do to help, Jack? We've got a lot of space to fill; we'll put in anything you like. We also have one hell of a library—it's at your disposal."

Stryker smiled down at him weakly. "We could try advertising for the bastard. 'Free offer—come in with your hands up and we'll give you a brand-new toaster oven plus a year's supply of waffles.' What do you think?"

"I think I feel sorry for you," Ballinger said. He looked at the others. "I think I feel sorry for all of you."

"Welcome to the club," Neilson said.

FOUR

STRYKER WOKE UP the next morning in a very bad mood.

It was not improved by the prospect of his court appearance at nine o'clock. That is, he was *called* for nine—the chances were he would hang around for hours and say nothing.

And then he couldn't find a parking space.

The courtroom was crowded with spectators who had fought their way in and were not prepared to leave. Reporters overflowed the press area and filled the outer hall, jostling with photographers both freelance and assigned, waiting for the arrival of the defendant.

Harry Bronkowsky was a big, bad man, and big, bad men are news—especially when they've been caught to rights on a Murder One charge. The judge was happy—he loved getting his name in the papers. The reporters were happy—they loved a juicy story. The DA was happy—he loved a certain conviction.

Stryker was not happy.

Nor was anybody else in the police department.

But the witness schedule said Lieutenant J.E. Stryker, and he had to tell his story, which was simple and vital to the prosecution, because it was Stryker and his team who had broken the case and made the arrests.

Not that they had enjoyed it—in clearing up the case they had also uncovered a dirty cop, and now the department was on trial in the media as much as the accused in court.

That there are rotten cops surprised no one.

The surprise is that there are so few of them.

Detective Lieutenant Tim Leary was one of the few.

When you deal with filth every day, when you see that filth enriching itself, living high and laughing, when you have so many opportunities to do the same, it is inevitable that some men falter, go over, go under.

There were many police officers attending Bronkowsky's trial in one capacity or another, and there wasn't one of them who hadn't transgressed, looked the other way over something small, given the benefit of the double where there was really no doubt, perhaps out of hope, perhaps for a favour done or paid for, perhaps out of laziness, perhaps even out of ignorance. It happens. But *they* had drawn their personal line. It wasn't always the same line, but it always said I go this far and no more. And they had stuck to it.

So they looked at Leary with the loathing of those who recognise something of themselves in another, with the zeal of reformed drunks who have triumphed over the bottle. They had stopped, he had not. Theirs was not a noble attitude, for mixed with their sense of justice was fear and self-doubt and the impulse, always, to protect the department.

They had caught Leary mouth open, hand out, and morals lacking. Big, balding, and wearing an eight-hundred-dollar suit, he claimed it was (a) a lie, (b) a mistake, (c) a one-off instance, and d) entrapment. It was the daily testimony of his former colleagues that seemed to anger him the most, and from his seat in the rear of the court he muttered frequently of what he could say about other cops, other scams, other broken trusts and honours if and when *he* was called to the stand.

As it happened, the district attorney was trying to avoid calling Leary to the stand. He might strengthen the prosecution's case by doing so, but putting him up there would also mean offering him to the defense for cross-examination, and that way lay all kinds of holes in the net for Bronkowsky's lawyers to jump through. It had happened several times before. This time the DA wanted Bronkowsky put away for good. So Leary stayed in the back of the court and glowered, his story untold, his self-justifications unexpressed. There would be time enough for those when his tribunal was called—but then the dirty linen would be hidden behind closed doors. Only the result would be made public.

Bronkowsky was on trial now.

And they were going to get him at last.

Stryker finished his testimony by eleven o'clock. As he went down the aisle, other cops who were testifying that day smiled at him sympathetically.

Leary wasn't one of them.

"NOW I UNDERSTAND," Kate said, half to herself, as the bus turned down what looked to her like a private drive but which proved to be a small country lane.

The man seated next to her turned his head. "I beg your pardon?"

"What Browning meant about being in England now that April's there—here. It's glorious."

He smiled, glanced beyond her at the passing landscape, and nodded. "It's glorious, all right—and *very*

unusual. Spring in England is usually just a slightly
warmer version of winter, which is wet, grey, and in-
credibly depressing. I admit, however, that when we
do it, we do it right.''

The coach rounded a curve and to right and left the
young green lawns of the village through which they
were passing were dotted with random swathes and
daubs of bright, clear yellow. ''And there are Word-
sworth's daffodils. I can't stand it,'' Kate said, knowing she sounded like a schoolgirl but unable to stop
herself. She had dreamed for years of coming to England and now she was here. Instead of the disappointment for which she had braced herself, there was
just what there should have been, everywhere she
looked. It was spring, it was England, and it was all so
right.

His smile became a grin. ''The weatherman says it's
going to continue. Mind you, he's usually wrong. You
may see the real England yet.''

''And that is?''

''Water, water everywhere, driving us to drink. I
daresay the per capita consumption of wellies must be
higher here than anywhere in the world.''

''Wellies?'' It must be some kind of drink, she
thought.

''I believe you call them 'gumboots.''' He pushed
his sliding glasses back into place and extended a
hand. ''I'm Richard Cotterell. And you are Kate Trevorne.''

She was startled. ''Yes. How did you know?''

''I asked. Immediately when I saw you this morning, I asked.''

''I'm flattered.''

"You should be—you looked absolutely dreadful. Jet lag?"

"Nightmares."

"If you tell me your dreams, I'll tell you mine. That is a threat, by the way."

She laughed. "Point taken." She looked out the window again.

"I understand you're going to be talking to us about Shakespearean murders."

"As if you didn't know about them already. I felt quite inadequate as soon as I heard the level of erudition at dinner last night. It's quite ridiculous to think an upstart American can tell any member of this august British gathering *anything* about Shakespeare."

"Piffle."

"My goodness—you actually say it."

"Piffle? In my tutorials I have used it frequently. I don't know about your students, but mine speak practically nothing else. Splendid word, piffle." He grinned again, causing all the lines of his face to curve upwards towards his dark blue eyes.

Kate gasped suddenly. "Oh, Lord—Richard Cotterell. I didn't make the connection. *In Love with Language*. It was absolutely *wonderful*—I've made it required reading for all my students."

"On behalf of my publisher, my agent, and myself, I thank you," he said, going pink across his cheekbones.

"Well, it isn't often someone bridges the great divide between academia and the real world," Kate said briskly, sensing his embarrassment.

"It was frowned on in some circles here," Richard said. "Not the done thing, you know, talking about language as if it might actually have something to do with everyday life.''

She chuckled. "I know what you mean. I teach two courses in crime fiction and there are some who think that's malarkey.''

"You really say it!" he said.

"Malarkey? Of course—it's American for piffle.''

He smiled. "So it is.''

They rode on in companionable silence. Kate glanced sideways at him. He was very attractive in a tweedy, bony way, with a good strong jawline and a touch of grey in his dark brown hair. She liked the shape of his head and hands, and the slow mellow sound of his voice. *Richard Cotterell, hey? Who would have thought it? I thought he'd be a prissy professor with a pince-nez and dandruff, and he's really quite young and—what was that English word I heard someone use last night?—ah, yes—he's really quite dishy.*

She settled back in her seat and looked out at the landscape she had longed for so many years to see. *Here am I, Kate Trevorne, an ordinary girl from the Middle West, sitting next to one of England's most famous academics, on a* bus *for goodness' sake, trundling along a rolling English road, with daffodils in the hedgerows and swallows in the sky, on my way to Stratford-on-Avon, where I am going to make a speech, about* Shakespeare *for crying out loud, to all these brilliant people. I must be dreaming. I must be out of my mind.* She glanced at Richard Cotterell's profile out of the corner of her eye. *And I must be sensible,* she concluded, turning back resolutely to the landscape.

They passed a bright, modern Texaco station, followed by a bright, modern shopping centre, followed by a bright, modern housing development. Oh, England, my England, stop before it's too late, she mourned. But that was selfish. People had a right to decent plumbing, easy shopping, and every convenience. The day she volunteered to live in a poky, dirty, dark but picturesque little cottage with an outside toilet—and leave it like that—would be the day she could demand that everyone else did, too. Then, as the coach rounded yet another corner, revealing an ancient pub with a thatched roof and pots of bright geraniums in the windows, she sighed with pleasure.

How very lovely it could be, and how grateful she was for every corner that had been kept that way.

After a while, Richard spoke again. "I think we should have dinner together tonight."

"Oh?"

"Yes. I think we should begin an Anglo-American exchange of piffle as soon as possible. Are you married?"

"No, but—"

"Neither am I, at the moment. I don't want to hear about the 'but,' by the way. You have to eat tonight, so do I—there is no earthly reason why we shouldn't eat at the same table, is there?"

"No, but—"

"I told you, I am not interested in 'but.' I am interested in you. Dinner—yes or no?"

"What happens if I say no?"

"I will cry out loudly. I will snivel and abase myself at your feet. I will ravel my sleeves. I will twine straws in my hair and eat worms, which I always carry with me in case of rejection. I will lie down in the aisle and

kick and scream all the way from here to Stratford."
He did not look at her, but kept his eyes on the back
of the seat ahead.

"Well," Kate said slowly. "We can't have that, can
we?"

STRYKER HAD BEEN at his desk for nearly an hour after lunch when Tos walked in carrying a file. "Hey,
you remember that drunk they found in the alley off
French Street a few days ago?" Tos asked, as he sat
down on the opposite side of the desk.

"Yeah." Stryker was deep in paperwork, as usual,
and hating it. All cops hate paperwork, but Stryker
hated it more than most, because doing it required him
to sit still for more than three minutes at a time. This
was against his religion.

"We had nothing on him, so we sent his fingerprints to Washington."

"Routine," Stryker muttered.

"Sure. We just got the report back. Guy's name is
Gabriel Lucas Hawthorne. Turns out he's on our
side."

Stryker wrote another two sentences before what
Toscarelli had said penetrated. He looked up to find
his friend regarding him patiently.

"The dead guy on French Street?"

"Yeah."

"He was a cop?"

"Sort of. Says here he was a federal investigator.
They're sending somebody over."

"I'll bet they are," Stryker said. "What the hell was
a federal investigator doing on French Street dressed
as a bum?"

"Well, now, I've got a theory about that," Tos said.

"You would," Stryker grumbled, and leaned back in his chair to listen. His chair creaked, and he sighed. Tos's face wore that peculiar expression he had when entering the realm of fantasy. Far off, and far in, the ancient face of the storyteller.

"Irresistible impulse," Tos pronounced finally. He looked as if this settled everything.

"You what?"

"Yeah." Tos leaned forwards. "He had an irresistible impulse to be a bum. Sort of a secret yen to stink and dress badly and stagger around in the street and fall down a lot. But he couldn't do it in Washington because somebody might recognise him, which would be embarrassing and probably bad for his promotion prospects, so he comes over here and tries it on. He likes it. It's wonderful—what he always wanted. No shining shoes, no brass hassle, just really scummy slobbishness. He stays. Then he—"

"Very funny," Stryker interrupted.

"You don't like my theory?" Tos was deeply hurt and he wanted Stryker to know that. He struck his chest with a soft fist.

"I *think* there might be another explanation," Stryker said wryly.

"Well, of course there's another explanation—but will it have any insight?" Tos wanted to know. "Will it have any flair?"

"Probably not."

"Well, there you are." Tos thought for a moment. He raised a finger. "What about leprechauns?"

"Leprechauns?"

"Say he was transported by leprechauns and—"

"I appreciate your efforts to brighten my day, but can we get serious here?"

"It is kind of funny, in a way, though," Tos said, leaning back. "It's another cop killing, isn't it?"

"How could it be? *We* didn't even know he was a cop—so how could the killer know?"

"No connection, hey?"

"Definitely not."

Tos grinned. "I wish you wouldn't use words like *definitely*—they make me nervous."

AT FIRST THEY FIGURED her for a lawyer.

Or a witness.

Maybe a victim?

How about a victim's wife?

Whatever—she made Neilson spill coffee all over his shoes, and even Pinsky turned his swivel chair for a look as she passed through on her way to Stryker's office.

About five foot nine, a leonine mass of deep red hair, and the kind of pale grey eyes that have a smoke ring of black around the iris. She wore a severely cut charcoal grey suit that did little to hide a voluptuous figure, black stockings ("O God," murmured Neilson), and slender high heels. She carried a briefcase under one arm and walked with the long, powerful strides of someone who probably ran ten miles every morning before breakfast.

"Lieutenant Stryker?" She held out a hand. "I'm Dana Marchant." She produced her identification. "I believe you have one of our people in your morgue." Her handshake was cool, dry, firm.

"Yes, so we've been told. I'm sorry."

"So are we. He was a good officer." Her tone made the standard tribute sound unconvincing.

"Was he Irish?" Tos asked, clearly unnerved.

"I beg your pardon?"

"Nothing," Stryker said hurriedly. "I believe his name was Hawthorne?"

"Gabriel Hawthorne, yes." She seemed to savour the names. "I'm assigned to work with you on the investigation. It's been okayed higher up." She unzipped her briefcase and produced a sheaf of print. "If you like, I can make the formal identification for the coroner. I worked with Hawthorne several times. He has no living relatives."

Stryker stared at her. What the hell was going on? The last thing he needed was to have this at his elbow when he was trying to work. She obviously had decided the case was now hers. He made a show of looking through the papers which, to his intense annoyance, were perfectly correct. "Please—sit down, Miss Marchant."

"Agent Marchant," came the brisk correction. "Thank you."

He went on reading, avoiding Tos's eye, which was suspiciously bright. He also, with some difficulty, avoided looking at the beautifully contoured knees which Agent Marchant exposed upon settling gracefully into the chair opposite him. "Can you give me any idea *why* Hawthorne would have been in Grantham?"

"None at all. I see that you had the case down as a probably mugging."

"And you don't agree?" He kept his tone even.

She shrugged her elegant shoulders. "I neither agree nor disagree. I didn't see the scene of the crime."

"Let's discuss it with the men who took the call." He raised his voice. "Neilson? Pinsky?"

Pinsky got up and began his slow amble across the room, but Neilson was in the door almost instantly, as if riding on well-greased roller skates. "Yes, Lieutenant?"

Stryker raised an eyebrow—Neilson rarely used his title or anyone else's below captain. "This is Agent Marchant, from the Justice Department. You and Ned caught the French Street homicide, didn't you?"

"The tramp last Sunday morning? Yes, we took the call on that."

"He wasn't a tramp. He was a federal investigator."

"No sh—well, for goodness' sake," Neilson said. "He certainly looked like a tramp to us. Good cover."

"The problem is not his 'cover,' Mr. Nelson," she said.

"Neilson, Harvey Neilson."

She looked him up and down briefly as he shook her hand. Neilson flushed under her scrutiny, and Stryker was reminded irresistibly of a young Roman matron assessing a new house slave. The woman had presence, he would give her that. He didn't feel inclined to offer anything else.

She was explaining things to Neilson, who was obviously ready to believe anything that emanated from those rosy, moist, perfectly formed lips. "His current line of investigation had absolutely no connection with this city, as far as we know. It involved corruption in and by certain so-called charitable organisations."

"No kidding." Neilson let go of her hand reluctantly. Pinsky had arrived and was leaning against the door, listening with half-closed eyes as he sucked on his empty pipe. He'd run out of tobacco that morning, and hadn't had time to buy any more. His homely crumpled appearance contrasted with Neilson's, who had combed his hair and put on his jacket the minute after Dana Marchant had passed by his desk.

"Agent Marchant has been seconded to us to aid in the investigation, Harvey," Stryker said carefully.

"Great," Neilson said. He beamed at her encouragingly.

"According to this letter, Washington feels that Hawthorne's death may be connected with the sniper who is picking off our officers."

"Ha!" Tos said, sitting up abruptly. "Told you."

"You know about that?" Pinsky asked, rather surprised.

"We have newspapers in Washington."

"Oh, come on!" Neilson said, somewhat desperately. "This is an entirely separate case." Already he could see his exclusive claim to her time slipping away. Stryker was chasing the police killings. "Nothing to do with the sniper."

"Not according to the ballistics report," Dana Marchant said.

"What did the ballistics report say, Harvey?" Stryker asked.

Harvey flushed. "I haven't had a chance to look at it. We've been working this other—"

Pinsky peeled himself away from the door frame. "I'll get it."

"I believe you'll find it was the same gun that was used to kill two of your policemen," Dana Marchant said.

"How did you get hold of the ballistics report?" Neilson snapped, embarrassed at being caught out.

She glanced up at him. "We can get hold of most things we *really* want, Mr. Neilson."

I'll bet you can, Stryker thought. He looked down and found himself staring at Kate's picture. Hello, honey, he thought. Why aren't you here protecting me instead of running around England being intellectual? Pinsky ambled back and handed the report to Stryker. "Looks like it *was* the same rifle that got the first two victims. They red-tagged the report but the tag came off apparently. Sorry, Jack, we should have caught it."

"Well, jeez—who would have thought some tramp being turned over had anything to do with—" Neilson began defensively.

"Was he turned over?" Stryker asked.

"Hell, yes—shot through the back of the neck and stripped of everything but his socks and jocks," Neilson said. "The bullet wound in itself wasn't fatal, but it opened some big blood vessels. Bannerman said he died of blood loss, but it was more or less a dead heat, you should pardon the expression, with freezing to death. Maybe that's why we didn't make the connection right away. Why should we? The guy was scabby, grimy—we figured a tramp, holed and rolled, right? We get maybe ten or fifteen like that every winter. It's rough down there. You *know* that, Jack."

Stryker looked at the woman and shrugged. "Under the circumstances, I would have called it a drunk roll, too, Agent Marchant. If it was our killer, then I'd guess that someone else stripped the body, sometime during the night. And most bullet *holes* look alike— until the ballistics report came through they didn't even know it had been a rifle." He glanced at Neilson. "Or course, if they'd read the thing sooner—"

She nodded. "I take the point." She sat quietly, thinking, and they all sat and watched her. Finally she looked up. "If you don't mind, I'd like to go to the morgue now."

"There's no need for that," Stryker said. "The official fingerprint identification from Washington is good enough."

"Oh, I *want* to do it," Dana Marchant said. She stood up and smiled, a wide, brilliant smile, full voltage on Stryker but the rest got some of the charge, too. "You see—I want to make absolutely *sure* Gabe Hawthorne is dead."

FIVE

"WHAT THE HELL, MCGUIRE?" Stryker demanded.

"Who's that?" came the cautious reply.

"This is Jack Stryker."

"Hi there," McGuire said, in a suspiciously jovial voice. "What's new?" McGuire was the local FBI co-ordinator, a marginally tolerable man Stryker had worked with before.

"You know goddamn well what's new," Stryker snapped. "We're having a problem with a sniper—"

"Yeah, I heard. Tough one."

"Right. Well, one of the victims turned out to be a visitor from Washington, name of Gabriel Hawthorne. Ring any bells?"

"It might." McGuire never gave anything away.

"Well, it did someone's, because the Justice Department sent over a liaison officer by the name of Dana Marchant."

A deep chuckle came down the line. "Now that *does* ring bells. What do you think of her?"

"Jesus—she's unbelievable," Stryker complained. "She looks like something out of *Vogue,* but she talks and acts like Granite J. Hardrock. Why didn't they just send me a nice guy in a Brooks Brothers suit?"

"If it's the outfit she usually wears, then it *is* a Brooks Brothers suit," came the gleeful reply.

"Come on, listen, a joke's a joke. Who should I talk to in Washington to get this changed?"

"Changed?"

"Yeah, dammit, changed. I want her out of here."

"Why? What's the problem? Count yourself lucky. She's as good as they come, Jack," was McGuire's reply. "They call her 'The Firebrand.'"

"I'll bet they do," Stryker grumbled.

"Got to you, did she?" McGuire said sympathetically. "I know the feeling. Thing is, Jack, the lady is all work and no play, despite the exterior decoration. I know—I've tried. We *all* tried when she was here once on assignment, but it's strictly business with her. They're beginning to say she's a dyke, but that's just the voice of bitter disappointment. She was married. Her husband died of cancer, and she has a kid of nine in a military school."

"What the hell has that to do with—"

McGuire rolled on. "My advice is, don't rock the boat, Jack. Tell her to ugly it up a bit if she's bothering you or your people. She'll understand. Some people think being beautiful is great—but it's a burden to her. You didn't see any makeup, did you? No fancy hairdo? The girl's straight, Jack, she can't help the way she looks. Hire the handicapped, that's what I say."

Suddenly Stryker realised what McGuire *thought* he was talking about. "It's not her *looks* that bother me, goddammit, it's her manner. As far as she's concerned, it's a dead heat between godliness, cleanliness, and her sweet ass."

"Oh right—I guess you mean she's using the Bossy Approach. Listen, we're all like that, Stryker," McGuire said in what he pretended was a soothing manner. "We see the big picture, we're take-charge guys, that's why we're in the Big People's Police, and not running around the boondocks with you local guys."

"I love it when you're obnoxious," Stryker snapped.

"Only trying to put things in perspective for you," McGuire said, no longer attempting to hide his amusement. "You're a real macho guy, aren't you? Yell at her, knock her around a little, she'll love it."

"Is that your only suggestion?"

"Do you really want me to answer that?" McGuire said, starting to chuckle.

Stryker told McGuire what he really wanted him to do, and slammed down the phone on what had become outright laughter. He considered complaining to Captain Klotzman, or even to the commissioner, but decided there wasn't much point in amusing anyone else with this. They wouldn't understand why he was upset. He wasn't quite certain, himself, he just knew it wasn't going to work. Agent Dana Marchant was beautiful, intelligent, able, and efficient.

And they were stuck with her.

DANA MARCHANT STEPPED OUT of the shower and blindly reached for the big towel that hung on the rail nearby. She wrapped a smaller one around her hair and walked, dripping slightly, into the hotel room. The television set was on, but turned down, so that the newscaster looked like a guppy in a square aquarium.

She sat on the edge of the bed and opened the pack of cigarettes she had bought downstairs after dinner. Gingerly she shook one out and lit it, coughing a bit, then settling to it.

Catching sight of herself in the mirror, she frowned. Not very clever to start again, when she had given up successfully six years ago. She took another drag, and then stubbed the thing out—tossing the rest of the pack into the wastebasket.

That wasn't the answer.

Any more than Gabe Hawthorne had been the answer, four years ago. "Bastard," she whispered, but it lacked conviction. Hawthorne hadn't been a bastard, just a guy on the make who had broken through her defenses because he was good-looking and persistent.

He hadn't been so good-looking on that slab.

She felt a tear rolling down her cheek and brushed it aside.

For a month he'd made her happy—give him that—and then he had moved on, saying that a month was all he gave any woman. Of course, until that ghastly moment she hadn't realised she *was* just any woman. All her life she had thought she was herself, unique, not one of a line of conquests. She'd honestly thought she'd found love again. Fool, she told herself. He didn't do it—you did it to yourself. And the anger and resentment you've felt ever since—you allowed that, too.

She'd been wrong to let it show this afternoon. Wrong to let her pain slip out. She knew that Neilson, the one who had taken her to the morgue, had noticed her reaction. He was young, savvy, attractive—and probably just like Gabe. Certainly he came on like Gabe, fast off the lip and ready for action. She was so sick of men who were "ready for action."

She wondered if Jack Stryker was like that.

Standing up, she spoke aloud. "No," she told herself. "No."

Since Hawthorne, Dana had kept herself on a tight leash.

Since Hawthorne she had thrown herself into her work.

Since Hawthorne she had been dead.

Now *he* was dead and the circle was complete.

She stood in front of the full-length mirror and let the towel drop to the floor. Her body was slim and shapely, long in the legs, narrow at the waist, full busted and hipped. It had felt no man's touch since Hawthorne's, and had wanted none.

Now she was remembering what it was like. And suddenly, she wanted to be in a man's bed again. To feel warmth, excitement, hunger, satiation. To feel what she had felt with Peter, her husband. To feel what she had tried to feel with Gabe Hawthorne.

Could she find it with Jack Stryker?

Stryker was so *alive*. Just like Peter had been. Something special ran in the veins of men like that, something extra in the blood, she was sure of it. It had hit her the moment she walked into his office, and although he didn't look anything like her late husband, there was the familiar impact of being in the room with someone dangerous, someone ready to spring.

Tiger, tiger, burning bright.

Damn, damn, damn.

"JACK?"

"Hi, Kate."

"Hi yourself, grumpy."

"Sorry—I was in the bathtub." He leaned over and grabbed his terrycloth robe, switching the phone from hand to hand as he struggled into it. Water ran down his legs and soaked into the bedroom carpet, and in the bathroom he could hear his nice hot bath gurgling down the drain—he'd caught the plug chain with his toe as he scrambled out to answer the phone. "So where have *you* been all night?" he asked, rubbing at his dripping hair with his sleeve.

"What do you mean?" Her tone was guarded.

"Well, it's about 3 A.M. there, isn't it?"

"Some of us had dinner together, then sat downstairs talking. You know how it is."

"Oh. Sounds like fun." There was a silence. He frowned. "Kate?"

"I had a bad dream," she said in a shaky voice.

He knew her "bad dreams." They were bone-shaking nightmares that reduced her to a small child whimpering in the night. He didn't know what they used to be like, but they were always the same now— him being shot or stabbed or thrown off the top of some tall building. He'd thought she was over it—she hadn't had any for quite a while. He sat down on the bottom of the bed. "I'm sorry, babe. Too far to hug."

"I know." She sounded very small.

"Have you met any of the other delegates yet?" he asked, trying to take her mind off it.

"Yes, most of them. They seem a very lively bunch. We've moved on to Stratford now." She gave him the number of the hotel. "Came on the bus—sorry, *coach*—this morning. Guess who I sat next to on the way?"

"Shakespeare?"

"No, silly—Richard Cotterell."

"Wow."

"*You* know, the one who wrote *In Love with Language*."

"Oh—*that* Richard Cotterell."

"All right, all right. I gave it to you to read, but I guess you never got around to it or you'd be impressed."

"I'm impressed, I'm impressed. What's he like?"

"Oh, very nice. Younger than I thought he'd be. Veddy English, you know—but nice." There was a pause. "I miss you. And I miss Pot."

He glanced over at Hercule Poirot, the black and white cat, thus named at eight weeks because of his magnificent moustaches, but nicknamed Pot because that's who he turned out to be. "Pot is fine, he is right here on the bed, washing his tail."

"Good. I hate missing you. Why couldn't you have gotten the time off?"

"I tried, didn't I?" But he hadn't tried very hard. The conference was her thing, her life. She'd have been busy and he would have sat around all day twiddling his thumbs. Better by far for them to go there together on a special trip that was all their own. Someday, maybe.

Theirs was an edgy relationship at the best of times. Sometimes he thought it might have been better if he'd fallen for some air-headed blonde who'd sit at home and knit him sweaters. And he was certain it would have been better for Kate to have loved some bespectacled professor with whom she could have long discussions about Proust. As it was, they pulled on opposite ends of the not-quite-marital rope—he in a job she hated and mistrusted, she in a world the impracticality of which occasionally exasperated him. They disagreed on almost everything, fought, struggled, and frequently despaired, alone and together. The only thing they shared was the deep need they had for one another.

It was her turn to attempt positive thinking. "What's happening back there, anyway?"

"Oh, the usual. Murder, rape, pillage, girl scouts selling cookies, reruns of 'I Love Lucy,' stuff like that. Oh, here's a twist. You remember that John Doe homicide on French Street last weekend? Turns out he's a federal investigator named Hawthorne, and that he was shot with the same gun as two of our victims. So they've sent over this hotshot to hound-dog us on the investigation. They think the whole thing should tie up, somehow. Neilson drinks in her every word, but I—"

"Her?"

"The liaison officer they sent us is a woman. Dana Marchant—apparently they call her The Firebrand."

"Why?"

This was getting dangerous; he should have kept his mouth shut. "I suppose it's because she's a redhead. Personally, I'd say the real reason is that she's a burning pain in the ass."

"But if she's beautiful—"

"Who said she was beautiful?"

"She must be—because you didn't say she wasn't." And this was a professor of English.

"I didn't say she was, either. What have her looks got to do with it, anyway?"

"Then she *is* beautiful—or Neilson wouldn't be so interested in her."

"Did I say he was interested in her?"

"Yes."

"Well, to me she's not so beautiful. Would you believe she marched into my office and tried to take over the case?"

Kate giggled. "Which you loved, I bet."

He sighed. Not even Kate could see his point. "I did not. She has no reason to think it's her case instead of mine. Only *one* of their precious investigators got knocked off."

"Oh, Jack—I wish . . ."

"That I was an insurance salesman. I know. I'm sorry. You get on with your work and I'll get on with mine, okay? I love you, you know. I also love me. I'll be careful." It took quite a while to reassure her, and he hated to think what the telephone bill was going to be like but, eventually and reluctantly, they hung up.

He padded downstairs, still dripping, went over to the bookshelves and scanned along them until he found what he wanted. *In Love with Language* by Richard Cotterell. He turned the book over and stared at the photograph on the back. How could she have thought he was old? A long, intelligent face under a thick mop of romantically tousled hair, a sensuous mouth curling around a pipe stem, tweeds and an open collar, long legs stretched out athletically as Professor Richard Damned Cotterell leaned against a fencepost and gazed into the middle distance.

Well, he hadn't *really* told her what Dana Marchant looked like, either.

He wondered if that made things even.

SIX

FRENCH STREET at 8 A.M. is not a sight to lift the heart—although if you are a police detective hoping to interview some drunks, the vista offered possibilities.

They were everywhere—huddled in doorways, curled up on heaps of plastic garbage bags, snuggled into dumpsters with the rest of the refuse. Of course, many more were living in flophouse luxury—a bed, a blanket, a place to throw up.

French Street had a very orderly progression of existence.

At dawn it was relatively quiet. Later on a few shops would open, always cautiously. Rents were low and chances of survival were slim, but people kept trying to sell aspirin and newspapers and bread and pickles and, of course, booze. Gradually the drunks would lurch forth pale and bleary, heading with slow determined steps towards the nearest liquor store or bar. Later still would appear the drug wholesalers in their dark limousines, rolling along the side streets slowly to set bait—supplying their pushers who would hang loose in their usual shadows, ready for customers with the "God! It's morning and a whole day ahead of me" blues. After five, the dark limousines would roll up again to empty the nets, count the catch, and replenish supplies of bait. By early evening the place would be jumping again. The tawdry strip bars and sex shops would flicker up their fluorescent fingers and beckon.

The patrolling pimps in their suits of lights and their spangled Caddies would roll the main line, checking out their girls, taking their cuts, and maybe making a few to keep discipline. In between all this twinkling high life would stagger the drunks, eyes glazed, mouths open, lurching from one bottle to the next, one doorway to the next, one handout to the next, neon flashing bright colour onto cheeks that had none, and shadows hiding the dirt and the fraying edges. The dream time, the all-right dark, the let's pretend.

But the mornings were cruel.

Stryker parked around the corner, on Delaney Avenue, and locked up tight. They walked to the end of the street and surveyed the vista of closed bars and boarded-up stores.

"I see what you mean," Dana Marchant said.

"You didn't have to come," Stryker snapped.

"Of course I didn't," she snapped back. "I could have stayed in my hotel and had a manicure. That would have accomplished a lot, wouldn't it?"

"Touchy, touchy," Tos said mildly. "Just because you're pretty doesn't mean you can forget your manners."

She looked up at him. "No?"

"No," Tos said.

She stared at him for a minute, then grinned up at him. "It's a little early in the morning for me. I work nine to five in Washington."

For a moment Tos wavered, then he broke, and grinned back.

"Not here," Stryker said, unamused.

"I'm not asking for favours, Lieutenant," Dana said. By the time her eyes reached his, the grin was gone. "Just the one—to do my job on your turf. I promise not to cry." She was dressed in jeans, boots, and a couple of thick sweaters under a pea jacket, a knitted cap covering her red hair. She still looked entirely female.

"And to think Rivera voluntarily spends his time down here," Tos said, shaking his head. "No wonder half the guys think he's a saint, and half think he's nuts."

"Who's Rivera," Dana asked.

"What they call a legend in his own time," Tos said.

"He's just a real good undercover cop," Stryker said impatiently. "Brilliant at taking on a character and sustaining it. He's got a new angle on this area, and they've let him do his own thing."

"We might run into him," Tos said.

"Yeah, and not recognise him," Stryker smiled. "His own mother wouldn't recognise him, some days."

"How do you want to do this?" Tos asked, shifting uneasily from one foot to the other. He hated this area, hated everything it was and everything it represented. His own father had ended up down here, and the memories of having to track him down, dry him out, and drag him home were the most horrific of his adolescence. When the old man had died there was more relief than sorrow in his mourning, but he never spoke of it. Even Stryker didn't know. "Split up or stay together?"

"They're too hung over to be dangerous," Stryker said.

"Do you want to rephrase that?" Tos asked. "How would *you* feel if you had a hangover, a bellyache, and low blood sugar, and some bastard cop shook you awake and asked you dumb questions?"

Stryker had slept badly the night before, and he nodded wearily. "Right, right—we'll take this side first. Together. Does that make you feel better?"

"Yeah. Not good, I don't claim good, but better."

"Wonderful." They moved along about ten yards, stopped at a drunk, then moved on. After viewing two or three, Stryker found what he was looking for. "And here we have our first customer, whose name I believe is Grunt, and who hails from the doorway of Sal's Bar-B-Cue, spit-roasted cardboard a specialty. Good morning, Grunt."

"Good morning, Grunt," Tos echoed.

Grunt opened one blazing eye. "Go shit yourself, Stryker," he said. "You and them both."

Stryker turned to Tos. "Well, we're in luck—Grunt seems to be in a good mood this morning."

"Swell," Tos said sourly.

"You know the guy who got killed here last Sunday morning?" Stryker asked the heap of rags. "How would you like to join him?" He reached out and dragged the man upright into a sitting position.

"What the hell?" Grunt pulled away from Stryker's grasp. "Are you rousting me or what?"

"There's a killer loose on French Street," Stryker said softly. "Maybe he's the kind of killer that likes to pick on street people, easy meat, for fun. For fun, Grunt. Want to be somebody's fun, Grunt?"

"Oh, for Christ's sake, stop with the Hollywood dialogue, will you, Stryker? You been watching too many B movies." Grunt unwound himself and shook his clothes into place, rubbing his face. "What the fuck do you want? Who's the broad?"

"Look at the picture." Tos held out the photograph of Gabriel Hawthorne.

"Okay, so I looked. What the hell time is it, anyway?" Grunt pulled off his ragged stocking cap so as to better pursue whatever it was that lived in his shaggy mop of hair. He shifted from one buttock to the other and gave a grimace of pain. "Goddamn, my balls are froze to the step."

"It's eight o'clock and all is not well," Stryker announced to the sky. He watched as the ragged man continued to groan and squirm with discomfort. "Are you serious?"

Grunt shook his head. "Naw—just felt like it for a minute there. Why, were you going to call a goddamn ambulance or something?"

Stryker, who had been caught off guard in a moment of startled sympathy, shook his head. "Tell me about the man in the picture."

"He's a talent scout for MGM. He promised me everything, said I could be a—did you say eight o'clock?" Grunt interrupted himself in a horrified voice. "You mean you woke me up with an hour to go before I can get a fucking drink? You bastards."

Stryker felt in his pocket and produced a miniature of whisky. He held it out in front of Grunt's filthy face. "Tell me about the man in the picture."

"Oh, Jesus, you're a decent man," said Grunt with heartfelt greed, and reached.

"The man in the picture," Stryker insisted, moving the little bottle away.

"I gotta look again," Grunt said, his eyes on the bottle. Tos interposed the photograph between it and his glittering eyes. "So now I'm looking again. Oh, him. Yeah, so?"

"What name did he give?"

"I forget."

"Too bad," Stryker said, straightening up and starting to replace the bottle in his pocket. He had brought several, to take advantage of the delay before the package stores opened.

"Frank, Frank, he said his name was Frank," Grunt said, his voice thinning with desperation. "That's what he told us and that's how we left it."

Stryker retrieved the bottle from his pocket. "Where did he put up?"

"At the Cot," Grunt said.

"Did he have much money?" Dana asked.

Grunt eyed her. "If he did I never saw it. I said he was frank, I didn't say he was stupid," he cackled. He looked at her, suddenly suspicious. "If he had money, why would he stay down here, girlie?"

Stryker handed him the tiny bottle, and added a ten-dollar bill to it. "Thank you and good morning."

Grunt, having finished off the miniature in one gulp, looked after them reproachfully. "What's this shit? I solve your whole damn case for you and all I get is a crappy ten spot?"

"You didn't tell me how many teeth he had, you didn't say the magic password, you didn't know the capital of Switzerland, you didn't—" Stryker called back over his shoulder.

"All right, all RIGHT!" shouted Grunt, who knew when he was beaten. "Next time I want fifty."

"Next time we'll ask somebody else," Tos said.

Grunt turned to a fellow alky who was struggling to his knees in the next doorway, his eyes on the miniature bottle. "See? See? You do good work and what thanks do you get?" With a grand gesture, Grunt tossed the empty bottle away. The alky scrambled after it, licked a drop from its tiny neck, and then put it carefully into some inner recess of his clothing.

"Thank you," said the alky, and sat back down again. "Thank you, thank you, thank you, thank you, thank you, thank—"

Grunt groaned. "Don't start up with me."

"Thank you," concluded the alky, and went back to sleep.

THE COT was the street nickname for the men's refuge run by a local charity. It was in a large building that backed onto a silted-up tributary of the Grantham River, and had formerly been a warehouse. It did a roaring business in the winter, but in the summer many beds were empty because the French Street drunks preferred sleeping rough to abiding by its curfew and rules.

They were strict. Off the street by nine, a supper of soup and bread while being read uplifting literature, in bed by ten-thirty, up again at seven to a breakfast of porridge, bread, and milky coffee, followed by an hour of cleaning duties before release again onto the street by nine. If you had slept there the previous night your hand was stamped as you left, so you could return for lunch—stew and bread and wash up your own dishes. The dishwasher contained a bleach which removed the ink of the stamp. (When the Cot had originally opened, they had issued lunch tickets, but when they discovered the tickets were being traded for booze money, they went over to the ink stamp. At first it was a picture stamp, but when they realized the men were washing dishes one-handed in order to preserve the stamp, they switched to a day stamp. When some men were discovered to be wearing gloves on the stamped hand to ensure a meal the following *week*, they switched to a progressive numbering system. And so the struggle continued.)

The Cot—more properly known as the French Street Men's Hostel—had been opened about two years before amid much publicity. The idea had been to provide a simple, regular pattern of life for those who wanted to break free of alcohol and the street. Many tried. Some succeeded. Most failed.

The great thing about it was that aside from the lunch-stamp system, no records were kept. Life at the Cot was strictly on a day-to-day basis, for the faces were always changing. Still, the man in charge, one Brother Feeney, had a remarkable memory. The Cot was not strictly a religious establishment, but it suited Feeney—origins, philosophical convictions, and outlook unknown—to dress himself in monklike garb. His was a nondescript face beneath a natural tonsure—growing baldness lending verisimilitude to his appearance. His floor-length habit of rough brown homespun was belted with a length of rope, and he wore sandals over thick, bright red socks. It seemed he must be fond of bright red socks, for several of his helpers sported them, too. Perhaps they had been donated by some company or other. There were signs all around that many of the things in the Cot had been donated by sympathetic companies or charities, and there was no doubt that Brother Feeney had gotten them all, from ballpoint pens to toilet paper, by the sheer force of his personality and his dedication to the cause of down-and-outs.

There was no doubt Feeney was eccentric, but he was clean, fair, and would listen to any man's trouble without judging him. If it had not been for Brother Feeney, the place would have fallen apart.

"Frank? Yes, I remember Frank." Feeney was scraping carrots for the stew which was bubbling in two huge cauldrons on the big stove in the kitchen. Around him several other men in more conventional garb moved, scrubbing, chopping, seasoning, stirring. The weather still being on the chilly side, they expected a good number for lunch. Feeney had told them, proudly, that the hostel had been nearly full the previous night. The current reading matter at the evening meal was *Moby Dick*—this had increased attendance considerably.

"Is he in some kind of trouble?" Feeney dropped the carrot he'd been scraping into the bowl and selected another from the heap.

"He's dead," Stryker said quietly.

The paring knife jerked. "Oh dear," Feeney said, wiping his bleeding hand down the side of his habit. "Poor man. He didn't seem ill at all. And he did not drink, I am certain of that."

"He was murdered, Brother Feeney," Tos said. "Shot to death, last weekend. It was at the other end of the street—didn't you hear about it?"

"I heard a man had been killed, yes. I didn't connect it with Frank at all, just assumed it had been a drunken argument. I think that's what somebody said, and I didn't pursue it. They're like children, you see, such strong passions, such rages. They don't think. They don't take *time* to think." He seemed genuinely upset. "I had hopes of Frank. He was an interesting person. Intelligent. He seemed very interested in the work we do here. He helped me out in the office quite a bit—I'm rather better at stews than bookkeeping, unfortunately. When he didn't come back, well—they don't, you know. They stay for a while and then—" He sighed deeply, and picked up another carrot. "I try not to think too much about what goes on outside. It's what happens in here I care about."

"When was the last time you saw him?"

Brother Feeney scratched his nose, still holding the paring knife, which went back and forth in front of his unfocussed eyes. "Let me see—you say he was killed on the weekend?"

"Saturday night or early Sunday morning," Stryker said.

"Yes, well—it was before that, you know. I would say it was the previous day, Friday, that he left us. I thought he had succumbed to the lure of Bacchus, to be honest. He'd come to us in a sober period, you understand, with the hope of making it last, but I thought he had weakened. Some are like that—two weeks dry and then off on another binge. I thought he was one of those."

"So you didn't see him after Friday?"

"That's right. Lunchtime at the latest."

"Did he make any particular friends here? Or enemies?"

Feeney shook his head. "No, not that I recall. He had an interest, a lively interest, but it was in everyone, if you see what I mean. He talked to a great many of the men; he was a very good listener. That's important in this work, you know, listening."

"In ours, too," Stryker said, closing his notebook.

"I DON'T KNOW what the hell they want to take her down to French Street for," Neilson griped as he and

Pinsky drove over to Richmond's house. "That's no place for a woman like her."

"She's a federal agent, isn't she?" Pinsky said. "She's been trained for things like that."

"Oh, sure—in a book and classroom kind of way. That's nothing like being a street cop, Ned. Federal investigators are all talk—when they want dirty work done, they call us half the time," Neilson said. "I mean, she probably did her college degree in psychology, did a quick stint at the sharp end so she could say she did, and then got transferred right out of the sunshine."

"She moves like she's pretty healthy," Pinsky pointed out. "I bet she works out, runs, something like that. You don't get that kind of free swing without doing some kind of sport—tennis, or fencing, or dancing, maybe."

"I'll tell you another thing," Neilson went on doggedly. "She was glad as hell to see that Hawthorne guy on a slab, you know? Said—just for identification purposes—does he have a small circular scar on his ass? And Bannerman turned him over and there it was. I bet *she* put it there. Probably bit him."

"Oh, come on."

"No, I mean it. You don't get that kind of smug look from grief. I bet they had a thing going and he dumped her, something like that."

"Does she look like the kind of woman who gets dumped?"

"Well, no—but who's to say whether or not this Hawthorne guy was some kind of creep who'd dump Miss America, for instance, hey? Some guys, they have the downs on beautiful women, like to make 'em feel like dirt."

"Not you," Pinsky observed, as Neilson pulled over to the curb and checked the number of the house against the one he'd jotted down in his notebook.

"No, not me," he agreed. "I appreciate loveliness in all its many forms—especially the female of the species. This looks like it, number 4584 Pacific Avenue."

THE LIVING ROOM of the small frame house was neat and clean, although the furniture was worn and there were traces of children everywhere. A tumble of toys boxed in one corner, a small odd slipper caught under the sagging springs of an armchair. The top of the television set was literally covered with framed snapshots of children, gap-toothed and grinning for the most part, different ages, sexes, and hair colours, but all with the same long jaw and wide-set eyes of the man opposite.

"I don't want to talk about it," Richmond said sulkily.

"Come on, man—this guy is blowing away cops," Neilson said.

"I *know*—I saw him do it." Frank Richmond was a lanky, hard-bitten man with traces of a Georgia cracker accent still lingering in the back of his throat. His clothes hung loosely on him, as if he'd lost a lot of weight. The skin of his face was pale and dry, and his hands shook as he lit a cigarette. "How'd you like to have your partner's brains all over *your* lap, hey? Listen, I'm still loyal to the department and all that, but I had to get out, you understand? Next time it might be me, and what brains I got I want to keep *inside* my head."

"That's why you quit, right?"

Richmond looked defensive. "Goddamn right. I didn't mind facin' 'em down, I didn't mind gettin' beat up, I didn't even mind gettin' spit on now and again. We all get that, we all got to put up with that. But gettin' mine from ambush, when I ain't got no chance to defend myself? Hell with that." He tapped his cigarette again and again on the edge of the ashtray, although there was no ash to fall. His nails were bitten to the quick.

"How did you get on with Randolph?"

"I got on with him fine. Just fine. He was a good boy."

"I understand he was black."

"Yeah, he was black. So?"

"That's not a Boston accent you've got there," Pinsky said quietly.

"Not everybody south of the Mason-Dixon line is stupid," Richmond said. He also spoke quietly, but there was an element of warning in the tone. "I grew up with coloureds, I know their worth. I was proud to stand beside Sandy Randolph anytime, anywhere, you just put that down in your goddamn book, okay? Put it down." His voice rose, thin and sharp, as if to defend himself from invisible attack.

"Okay, okay—take it easy," Pinsky said. "Sorry."

"He was a good-looking kid, too," Richmond went on angrily. "The bastard blew his face away, his wife couldn't even look on him before she buried him. That's what got me. His wife, Clemmie, hurtin' so bad she couldn't even cry, just stood there at the funeral, like a black statue, and their first baby still in her belly. He never even saw his daughter. I got four kids, and I don't want my wife standin' in the rain over my grave getting con-so-lation from Commissioner Moorhouse sayin' what a great cop I was. I wasn't. I was just an ordinary cop, did my best, that's all. Sandy— he was getting there. He was getting good. But not on the street. He wasn't really hard enough for the street—he was leavin' the street. Goin' on that new computer course the federation set up, do administration. Could have been the first black chief we ever had, now he's..." Richmond stopped as suddenly as he had started. "Now he's dead," he finished, bitterly. He was a skaken, beaten man.

Mrs. Richmond appeared with mugs of coffee on a tray. She was a small, faded woman with large, luminous eyes. There was a plate of homemade cookies on the tray as well. "I thought y'all might be peckish," she said shyly. She made as if to leave the room, but Richmond reached out as she went. He said nothing, but held her hand to his face. She stroked his hair, as if he were a child, then smiled over his head at them, as if in apology. When she had gone, Richmond avoided their eyes. He picked up a mug, stirred in sugar from the bowl, and gestured to them to help themselves. He held the mug in both hands, as if to draw its warmth into his body.

"What was the call?" Neilson asked.

"Sorry?"

"The call you were on when—" Neilson gestured vaguely with his mug, nearly spilling some on the rug.

"Oh. Arson. Somebody set some itty-bitty fires in the basement of a condemned building, real amateur stuff, but if it's arson the fireboys have to call us, so we went. Kids, we figured, it was so dumb, kerosene everywhere and newspapers crumpled up. Call went in before it hardly took—they wanted to hear the sirens, see the engines roll up. We took the details from the fireboys, then started back.''

''The fire was where?''

''In them tenements—you know the Gallo district?'' When they nodded, he nodded back. ''In them tenements on Evergreen. We were headin' back on Polk when this car overtakes us, and the driver lifts up his arm and blows Sandy's brains out.'' His face was stiff, as if he were afraid a show of emotion would shatter it, and a pulse was beating at temple and throat. He swallowed, sighed, looked away. ''This is all in my report. I did all this before.''

''The story is, we have to start again, from scratch. Before your interview was local—we're downtown,'' Pinsky said. ''It's a bitch, but there you go. We got your reports, they're real clear and all that, but we just wanted to hear your impressions for ourselves. Something extra might come back, now, some little thing.''

''I been tryin' to forget it, not remember.''

''We want the bastard—don't you?'' Neilson burst out.

Richmond stared at him bleakly. ''I did. Our preacher, he says I shouldn't be vengeful, so I'm tryin' not to be. It won't bring Sandy back, or them others.''

''No, but it might stop him before he kills any more!''

''Yeah, you're right, I know you're right.'' Richmond sighed—his defenses seemed suddenly exhausted. ''I didn't hardly see him, he was on the other side of Sandy, you know? Sandy was drivin', I was on the radio, when this Camaro pulls alongside. Black Camaro it was. And the sun was coming from behind it, so the guy was just a dark blob inside. Sandy cursed because the guy was crowding him and there wasn't a lot of room, and then the guy lifted his hand and the sun caught a glitter off the gun and then there was blood everywhere and we went into a wall and that was it. I don't remember anythin' until wakin' up in the hospital all strapped up. They didn't tell me about Sandy, they didn't say nothin' about him—that's how I knew he was dead. Knew right away."

"You said Randolph wasn't 'hard enough' for the street," Neilson said. "What do you mean, exactly?"

Richmond shrugged. He was wearing a beige V-necked sweater over what had been a pale blue uniform shirt, and the wool of the sweater caught on the nap of his chair's upholstery, giving him a lopsided appearance as he sat there. "Sandy was always reading books on psychology and sociology and all that stuff. Show him a kid caught cold with a crowbar in one hand and the other in the till and he'd try to 'understand' him instead of arresting the little bastard. We had some go-rounds about that—couple of times he—well—he 'used his judgement,' you know?"

"Sometimes that's good policing," Pinsky said mildly.

"Maybe sometimes, yeah. Maybe others, no. Not when you know the little sons 'a bitches are just going to go around the corner and do it again, right? They laughed at him, but he never saw it. Give him his due, he was *beginning* to see it. The Gallo district isn't exactly Bloomsbury Hills, after all. Day after day out there, you learn what's what and what isn't. Not that it matters, now."

They sat in silence for a moment.

"This dark blob in the other car—could you see anything about him at all?" Pinsky asked.

"Nope—he was just a blob, a what d'ya call it—a silhouette."

"Broad shoulders or narrow?" Pinsky asked, putting his empty mug back on the tray and taking another cookie. "Was the silhouette wide or narrow?"

Richmond's eyes narrowed. "Wide," he finally said.

"Short neck or long?" Pinsky said, his mouth full.

Another pause. "Long."

"Shape of head?"

"Round. No—solid, more square than round."

"And the top of it?"

Richmond's eyes opened up—he was no longer focussing on his memory, but on Pinsky's face. "What do you mean, the top of it?"

"Was it fuzzy or smooth?" Neilson said calmly. "Did he have hair or was he bald? Or was he wearing a hat?"

Richmond grinned suddenly. "He was wearing a cap, goddammit! When he was facing forwards you could see the peak, and then when he turned, there was just the shape of his head. If it had been a hat, the brim would have stuck out, whether he was facing sideways or frontwards, right?"

Pinsky leaned back and inserted the remains of the cookie into his mouth. "Right," he said.

"Son of a bitch," Richmond said. "I never thought of it before."

They went on talking to Richmond for another twenty minutes, but aside from that one detail, they got nothing new from him. When they emerged, Pinsky was pleased.

"Well, we got that about the cap," he said.

Neilson looked at him with some degree of pity. "Ned—there are eight million caps in the naked city. That was just one of them."

SEVEN

"WHO ACTUALLY OWNS the Cot?" Stryker asked his spaghetti carbonara.

"Some church or something, probably," Tos answered, when the pasta declined to reply. "It's not Catholic, though—I'd know if it was Catholic."

"I think we should check it out," Stryker said, passing the parmesan cheese to Dana. "Because from what Brother Feeney said, Hawthorne was checking it out."

"What makes you say that?" she asked, sprinkling cheese on her ravioli.

"Don't you remember? He said Hawthorne talked to all the men. He said he volunteered to 'help out' in the office."

"I thought the Cot didn't keep records," Tos said. "No names, nothing like that. It's why the bums figure they can go there and not get hammered."

"Oh, they don't keep records of the men who stay there, no. But they must keep records of everything else—expenditures, personnel, stuff like that. My guess is, he was trying to run down who financed the place, maybe. Who had an interest."

"Why should he do that?" Dana asked.

"Because—I don't know. Because there's something funny about it? Didn't you say he was working on corruption in charitable institutions or something like that?"

"Yes—but what's that got to do with your sniper?"

"What's our sniper got to do with Washington?" Stryker countered. "Maybe nothing, maybe everything. Maybe the killer figured Hawthorne for a cop because he was asking questions. In which case, God help all cops. Either Hawthorne got too close to what he was after on the charity thing and had to be killed—in which case, why by that person with that gun? Or he was investigating his charity thing and got killed by that person with that gun for some totally different reason. Until we get that out of the way, we won't know for sure which trail to follow."

"This is a hunch, right?" Dana asked.

"Yeah, this is a hunch.":

"A hunch is what you're sitting in," Tos pointed out. "Sit up straight or you'll get an ulcer."

"I *have* an ulcer."

"There you go, then, it's only proof," Tos said complacently, digging into his salad. "You should sit up straight, drink lots of water, chew thoroughly. Masticate, irrigate, masticate, irrigate. Like that."

"So you keep telling me," Stryker said resignedly.

"Do I look bad on it?" Tos asked of Dana. "Do I?"

She took her time evaluating his appearance. Six foot two, about 190 well-distributed pounds of bone and muscle, gleaming thick black hair, clear complexion, bright eyes, perfect teeth.

"I must confess, you look well," she conceded.

"He got like that stuffing pasta down his gullet for the first thirty-two years of his life," Stryker revealed, with some irritation. "Plus genetics. He only started on this health kick a few years ago. Since then he's had pleurisy twice *and* appendicitis with complications, to say nothing of two sprained ankles."

"You can't count the ankles," Tos said. "That was ice."

"That was retribution," Stryker said. "For all the crap you keep giving me. Masticate, irrigate, pontificate—that's you. Pass the salt."

"Poison, pure poison," Tos said. "Leave it alone."

"How would you like a faceful of dangerous spaghetti?"

Tos handed him the salt. "Don't blame me," he said.

"The case Hawthorne was chasing involved a very particular charity," Dana said slowly. "The Abiding Light Association. There was some question of payoffs to a few corrupt IRS officials not to pursue investigations involving certain establishments thought to be funded by Abiding Light. A couple of gambling houses, a brothel, a smuggling network, a drugs factory—stuff like that. From the protection they get, I figure the people behind Abiding Light are pretty powerful, but we've never been able to trace them. If Gabe got onto the end of some thread that led back here—"

"You might have mentioned this little item before," Stryker said, trying not to grind his teeth.

"I know—sorry. But the fact that he was shot with the same gun as the others . . . sort of confused the issue. It still could be completely unconnected, you know."

"I know, I know," Stryker said, scraping up the last of his spaghetti with a piece of bread.

"What would you like me to do?" Dana asked.

He was pursuing an errant piece of smoked ham with the last piece of crust. "Go back to Washington."

"I see."

He looked up and shook his head. "No, you don't. Go back to Washington and get hold of everything you can that Hawthorne was working on. Clear his desk, check out his files, all of it. And bring it back here. If we can figure out what brought him here, we might find what killed him here. Either that, or it will eliminate the connection. Can do?"

"Are you sure this is necessary?" Her voice was cold.

"Very certain. You must see the logic of it."

"Oh yes—it's *logical* all right," she conceded.

"Well, then—go," Stryker said.

She glanced up at the clock. "Can I have my zabaglione first?"

Tos closed his eyes and shook his head. "Eggs, cream—I can hear your arteries clogging."

Dana's glance met Stryker's. "Does he always go on and on like this?"

"All the time."

"Do you ever get the impulse to kick him?"

"All the time."

"What stops you?" she asked with some curiosity.

He looked at his partner, looming large on the other side of the booth. "I'm afraid he might fall on me," Stryker said.

"I THINK WE'RE BEING talked about," Kate said, watching two swans glide past on the silvery Avon, twinned by their reflections.

Richard Cotterell stretched out under the tree and stared up through the branches at the intense blue of the Oxfordshire sky. "Does that worry you?"

"In a way, yes. It makes me think I should pull myself together and stop giving in to your every invitation. We keep seeing sights and missing lectures."

"As you Americans would say, I 'majored' in Blandishment, followed by Advanced Lures, and Higher Level Temptation. I have a degree in Comparative Cajolery, as well, but I don't talk about it as it was only an honorary degree awarded by the Nether Wallop College of—"

"Oh, shut up."

"—Animal Magnetism and Upholstery. Are you very much in love with him?"

"With whom?" Kate picked a small daisy and turned it round and round between her fingers, making its head spin.

"Oh, good—you've forgotten his name already."

"Of course I'm very much in love with him. That's the trouble. The only thing we have in common *is* being in love. He's all flash and zap, I'm all sit around and contemplate. He goes for a brisk two-mile run after dinner, while I sit and do patchwork or correct essays. He loves being in danger, I panic when a door slams unexpectedly."

"From what you've told me about your recent experiences, I'm hardly surprised."

"Yes, well—that's another thing. People who fall in love because they've endured some horrible experience together don't always last together. In the clear light of day—"

"It's a clear day today," he pointed out as he sat up. "Last night, together, we endured a ghastly pair of speeches and some quite execrable cuisine. Do you still love me?"

"Don't be stupid." She felt herself flushing. "You're only behaving like this because the conference is so boring."

He sighed. "God, it is, isn't it?" He glanced at the programme that had been folded in his pocket. "This evening we can choose between 'Shakespeare the Feudalist—the Socio-Economic Structure of Elizabethan Drama,' or 'Shakespeare's Virgins—A Marxist Feminist Critique.'" He peered over it. "Did you know there is a town not very far from here called Broadway, and in that town there is a hotel with a dining room that will take you back to England as we like to think it used to be but probably never was. How about it?"

Kate shrugged and looked away towards the river. "I don't think so, Richard. Thanks, anyway."

"Denying your own pleasures—that's a good sign. You feel guilty, and you wouldn't feel guilty if you weren't tempted, would you?"

"A very Jesuitical argument. And I don't feel in the least guilty."

He went into reverse mode, shrugging his shoulders negligently. "Please yourself, young Kate. Personally, I have no scruples where a rare baron of beef is concerned. If you don't come, I shall go alone and thoroughly enjoy the crisp roast potatoes, the exquisite Yorkshire pudding dripping with onion gravy, tiny buttered carrots, tender young asparagus, and afterwards a cream-laden brandy trifle that—"

"Oh, all right, all *right*," Kate laughed. The food at the hotel was truly awful, and she was starving.

"You can always tell a real woman by her appetite," Richard gloated. "We'll give our regards to Broadway. And then—"

"And then we will come straight back here and attend an evening lecture," Kate said firmly.

He stood up, caught her hands and drew her up and to him. He looked down into her face. "Maybe we will—maybe we won't," he said. "You haven't decided yet."

EIGHT

"A *CAP?*" Tos asked in dismay. "You talk to this guy for two hours and all you get is a *cap?*" They were sitting in Stryker's office, waiting for him to return from the john.

"That's all there was *to* get, Tos," Pinsky said. "We're lucky Richmond remembered that. He's a shattered man, he doesn't *want* to remember. Your partner gets blown away, there's more to it than just another goddamn murder, you know."

"Yeah, I know," Tos agreed morosely. "But a cap." He separated the toes of his shoes, which were resting on his desk, and peered at Pinsky through the gap. "What kind of cap?"

"A cap cap."

"Baseball cap? Golf cap? Jockey's cap? What?"

"Flat, with a short peak—like those tweed things Englishmen wear," Neilson said. "Gentleman's country cap."

"This is no gentleman," Tos said.

"So it was a disguise," Neilson said. "Normally he wears a flowered straw with a veil, and this time he thought he'd fool us. What a clever guy."

Tos didn't even bother to tell him to shut up. He just sighed and gazed up at the ceiling, his hands folded across his belt. "Well, while you were talking to Richmond, we were over at Santosa's precinct trying to get a line on *him*. We didn't get that much ourselves," he conceded. "We interviewed some of the people who worked with Santosa. Just another rookie, they said. A little timid, maybe. That's why they put him out in the boonies—he got reprimanded for failing to pursue a suspect on a bust. He froze, apparently, just stood there and let the guy get away over a wall. So his captain figured a few months being bored but safe might give him some guts, you know?''

''Works, sometimes,'' Neilson conceded. ''Walk around feeling big and being nice to old ladies and kids, lets you settle in.''

''And he gets shot,'' Pinsky said bitterly. ''Great move.''

''Well, hell—how were they to know? That's a fancy neighbourhood out there,'' Tos said. ''Nobody on the street at the time, everybody inside minding their own business, just sitting around being rich, so there were no eyewitnesses, nothing. They heard the shot, came out, there he was, bleeding all over their nice clean sidewalk.''

''Nice neighbourhood—where a uniform sticks out like a sore thumb,'' Pinsky pointed out. ''He was the first one who got it, remember. Maybe that was it—he was high profile.''

''You think order has something to do with it?'' Tos asked.

Pinsky shrugged. ''I don't know. I've been trying to think of anything I can. I even got to thinking about initials, you know? Like the ABC murders. Santosa, Trask, Randolph, Yentall—S,T,R,Y—I was waiting for the next one to be K and then maybe finding out it was Jack writing his name in blood or something, right?''

"I never heard of the ABC murders," Neilson said in some confusion. "Was that an old-time case, or what?"

"Agatha Christie," Pinsky said dismissively. "So then I thought time of service, right? First, we got a rookie, then a woman with two years' experience, then a black with three, then a detective with sixteen. It's a progression of a kind."

"You're forgetting Hawthorne," Stryker said, coming in and dropping into the chair behind his desk. "Hawthorne was not in uniform, not near a station house."

"That makes it even worse," Neilson said to Pinsky, grabbing a pencil and paper and making notes. "Now you got an H to put in, there. SHTRY? STRYH? HSTRY? How about History? Maybe there's an 'i' missing, somewhere, maybe some dead Ichabod or Inchworm that you and Agatha overlooked—"

"Forget it," Pinsky said, going a little pink.

"Who's Agatha?" Stryker asked. "Do I want to know about this line of reasoning?"

"No, you don't," Pinsky said. "Really."

Stryker looked at Tos, and Tos grinned and shook his head.

"You're sure?" Stryker asked, all innocence.

"Sure," Tos said, with a repressive look at Neilson, who was ready to outline the whole thing.

"We don't know much about the woman, yet—Merrilee Trask," Pinsky went on quickly. "And what about Yentall? Here's a guy, good cop—"

"Sloppy cop, they said. Sloppy reports, sloppy casework," Neilson put in, balling up the paper on which he had been jotting initials and lobbing it into

Stryker's wastebasket. "Neilson scores! The crowd goes wild!"

Tos shrugged. "We all make mistakes, Neilson, even you."

"Never," Neilson said with a wry grin. "Me, I'm perfect." He looked back into the outer office. "Where's the little red sexpot? Did somebody steal her in French Street, or what?"

"I've sent Agent Marchant back to Washington to pick up on everything Hawthorn was into, so we can find what brought him here in the first place. While she's doing that, we can work on local connections." He explained about the Abiding Light Association.

Neilson grinned. "Get thee behind me, Satan," he chuckled. "Or wherever."

Stryker looked at him. "What's that supposed to mean?"

Neilson shrugged and grinned. "She is some woman—kind of takes a guy's eye off the ball. If you know what I mean." He looked around at the others and gave a conspiratorial wink.

"No, I damn well don't, Neilson. Like to explain?" Stryker flared.

"Hey, hey, sorry I spoke," Neilson said. "Didn't mean to hit a nerve."

"Harvey, someday you're going to get into real trouble," Tos said, swinging his legs down from the desk and flexing his ankles.

"What did I do?" Neilson asked, all innocence.

"You pushed," Tos said, and kicked the leg of his chair so Neilson lost his balance, and had to grab the desk to stop himself going down.

"Now, listen—" he began angrily.

"All right, all right," Stryker said quickly. "Let's leave Hawthorne for the moment. We haven't come up with anything new on our cops, have we? Computer find any common arrests, stakeouts, operations?"

Pinsky shook his head, averting his gaze from his partner's angry glare across the desk at Toscarelli. He wondered how long it was going to take Neilson to grow up. It had been obvious to him and to Tos that Stryker was attracted to Dana Marchant and it had made Jack irritable and edgy. The fact that you could see it a mile off didn't mean you had to *say* anything about it. Stryker had been quite a tomcat before he met Kate, and old habits die hard, even when you find what you've been looking for. As far as that goes, his own eye had wandered a few times since he married Nell, so what? Your feet don't necessarily follow where your glance goes, and anyway, it was none of Neilson's business. Jealousy is what it was, what it came down to, in the end. Neilson had the hots for the redhead, and he knew that if Stryker chose to cut him off and move in on the girl, he could do it with no trouble, because the girl was interested, too. That, also, was visible a mile off. That's what got Neilson. That's what *really* got him. Neilson admired Stryker, and wanted to be like him, so there was always an element of competition in his actions. As if he wanted to prove something to Stryker, or to himself.

Pinsky answered Stryker's question in a neutral voice. "So far, we've come up with nothing that they had in common. Absolutely zip."

"Damn," Stryker said. "Okay—let's look again. They were all killed while on duty, except Yentall, who had just come off. They were all honest cops, and they all had clean records."

"Santosa had a reprimand," Neilson reminded him, rather sulkily.

"Right—but aside from that, clean records, yes?"

They all nodded.

Stryker stood up and began to walk around. "Okay, okay—what else? Any other angle we got on them?"

"Pinsky thought term of service," Tos said, before Neilson could get his mouth around ABC. "There's a progression there—so it might be history, common history. Something during training?"

"Told you it might be history," Neilson hissed in Pinsky's ear. Pinsky brushed him away as if he were a persistent mosquito.

Stryker nodded. "Maybe. Has anyone given their profiles to the shrink?" He looked around. "Do that. And talk to the administrator of training, look at their marks, position in graduating class, all that crap." He stood in front of the window, looking down at the street, his hands shoved in his pockets. Suddenly he pulled one out and made a mock swipe at the window, as if intending to put his fist through it, then turned back to them. "What about someone inside the department?" he asked quietly. "What about another cop?"

"Jesus, what an idea," Pinsky breathed.

"But why?" Tos asked.

"Grudge?"

"Oh come on," Pinsky said. "Santosa had only been working a couple of months, to start with. What kind of a grudge could anyone have against some rookie, for Pete's sake?"

"Maybe it was mistaken identity. Are there any other Santosas in the department?"

"Nine," Neilson said. "We checked them out. No relation, and no connection that we could discover."

"Well—the victims were on calls, some of them, weren't they? How about somebody in Central Despatch? Sending Trask to an abandoned car, and Randolph and Richmond to some amateur arson job..."

"Which the guy in Despatch had run out and set during his coffee break?" Pinsky asked. "Come on, Jack, you're scrabbling here. They didn't know each other, they never served together—"

"But someone could have served with all of them in turn," Stryker said. "We could check that out."

"Hell, yes," Neilson said, waving his arms in the air. "Excuse me while I take a week off just to work out the question for the computer, much less get the answer. Have you any idea what kind of checkup that would take?"

"It should be done," Stryker said stubbornly. "Tell somebody to do it, Harvey."

"Okay, okay, I'll tell someone to do it," Neilson conceded in the face of Stryker's determination to find a lead, any lead, going anywhere.

Stryker kept walking around the room, head down like a bull at a gate, angry and angrier. Suddenly he exploded, kicking the desk so hard it skidded a foot across the linoleum, leaving a gouge under each leg. "The only thing they have in common is the son of a bitch who offed them, dammit! Who is it?"

There was a silence.

Nobody said anything, until Stryker had moved the desk back and then thrown himself into the chair behind it, glowering at the paperwork which had been dislodged into new and more confused heaps.

"He wears a cap," Tos said.

"You what?" Stryker asked wearily. His outburst had exhausted his anger, and he felt foolish. They explained. They fell all over themselves explaining, but the whole thing fell on dulled ears. "A cap?" he asked, slowly, when they had finished. "You mean you talked to an eyewitness for two hours—"

"I *did* that number," Tos interrupted.

"And it wasn't a uniform cap," Pinsky said.

"Fine, fine," Stryker said in a tired voice. "Tomorrow we'll start checking out all the shops in town that sell caps."

Nobody believed he meant it.

The moment had passed. Stryker's anger, the day wasted in fruitless interviews, the lack of inspiration—all conspired to bring them to a state of complete frustration. They discussed the cap angle for a while, but had to let it go. Once you'd said it, you'd said it. Cap.

"Well, this is great," Stryker said bitterly. "Looks like we'll have to put guards on all the cops in the city, wait for the bastard to kill again, and jump him in the act."

Nobody liked that idea either.

"Hey—maybe Dana will come up with something," Neilson said, trying to cheer everyone up. "Well, it could happen, couldn't it?"

"Put on your parachute, Harvey," Tos said. "If she does, it will be the day that pigs can fly."

NINE

DANA LEANED BACK against the seat and looked at her own reflection in the tiny window beside her. Well, here we are again, you and I, she told herself. Racing with the moon to get back to Grantham, carrying your little treasure in your hand and hoping for a word of approval from the goddamn King of Detectives. My God, you are a fool. You'll have to wait until morning, anyway, so why did you rush to catch the six o'clock shuttle? You tell me, she mouthed to herself. Except you already know, don't you?

There had been nothing in Hawthorne's files that gave any indication of why he had suddenly decamped to Grantham. She had searched his office thoroughly, with no result. Then she had talked with his secretary—and again, no result.

Gabe Hawthorne had always been a close-mouthed bastard, gathering information, putting a case together, waiting until he had the whole caboodle before theatrically springing it on an unsuspecting and dazzled audience.

It was how he had gotten results. And it was how he had gotten all the credit for those results.

Finally, she had gone through his desk. A hastily scribbled note, balled up and tossed into a drawer was all she came up with. On it, the following:

Grantham
French Street
Officer Higley

Immediately she had rung the Grantham police department, and asked them to locate Officer Higley for her. The answer had come back quickly enough— there was no Officer Higley employed by the Grantham police department. She then turned to the FBI's own computer and learned the only Officer Higley working in any police department anywhere in the country was a fifty-nine-year-old deputy sheriff in New Mexico who was due for retirement in six months. When she had phoned him, he said he didn't know anybody named Gabriel Hawthorne, but he had known a Maudie Hawthorne back in Virginia when he was a boy, but she'd be over a hundred years old now, was that any good?

Dana said it wasn't, but thanks anyway.

She had, as a last resort, pulled Gabe's confidential personnel file—and there it had been.

Gabe Hawthorne had been *born* in Grantham. He had grown up there, gone to school there. *And had joined the police department there.* He had, however, only served one month on the force when his father's company had transferred to Chicago, and he had taken the rest of the family with him. Gabe had only been nineteen, and still living at home. He'd taken an apartment, but two months later he'd resigned and followed his family to Chicago. His reason for leaving had been an argument with another officer named Higley, who also left the department at that time. Reading between the lines, Dana sensed that they had been allowed to leave rather than be kicked out. Gabe had gone to college in Chicago and gotten a law degree, and from there he had progressed into the Justice Department.

Now, after all those years, Gabe Hawthorne had
gone back to Grantham. And had died there. Why?
Why?

"Coffee, miss?"

Dana was startled out of her reverie. "What? Oh,
sorry—no thanks, no coffee."

"Tea? A cold drink?"

"Nothing, thank you."

The stewardess moved on, pushing her cart up the
narrow aisle. Dana moved on, too, with thoughts of
Jack Stryker.

She closed her eyes and tried to summon up his im-
age. Compactly built, broad forehead and level blue
eyes, a face startlingly young and alive under that
prematurely white hair, long straight nose and a firm
but sensitive mouth. He always seemed angry with her,
but she was certain he had a capacity for laughter as
well as tenderness.

Tiger, tiger, burning bright.

No. He was just another man. And not at all responsible for her response to him. He hadn't set out to
arouse this interest, and he certainly did nothing to
encourage it. After all, he had someone. She had seen
the woman's photograph on his desk. Short, dark,
curly hair. A heart-shaped face, with high cheekbones and a small, softly shaped mouth. Not conven-
tionally beautiful, but who, once seen, would be
remembered. A good match, probably, for his elec-
tric presence.

He had someone.

Someone he might be with right now.

They might be together right now.

She shivered and sat up, blinking.

"You always feel cold when you doze off like that," the elderly man next to her sympathised. "Would you like part of my blanket?"

STRYKER GLARED at the microwave and willed it to turn his frozen dinner into something wonderful. Slowly a bubble rose at the edge of the glass casserole, and then collapsed. The turntable went on turning, and, after a second or two, another bubble rose and fell.

Some things take a long time to thaw.

Some things melt at once.

He wondered what plane Agent Dana Marchant was taking back from Washington, and whether she would bring with her a new lead, a new insight, anything that would give them a way into or out of this goddamn mess.

He wondered what she was wearing, the Brooks Brothers suit and the black stockings, or the jeans and bulky sweater.

Either way, he should be thinking about something else.

Some choice—either think about cops going down all over the goddamned town, or think about Dana Marchant's ankles, knees, and all points north.

Turn on the television, he told himself.

Get involved with the world, you stupid putz.

He found it hard to believe he had ever enjoyed living alone. Hunched over a semicooked casserole in front of the television set, he felt like biting chunks out of the furniture instead of the rubber chicken and noodles. Wine, that was it. Open a bottle of wine. Enjoy yourself. Pour out a glass, put some Ravel on the stereo, pick up a good book.

Get drunk.

Get maudlin.

Throw up.

The hell with it.

By the time the telephone rang, he was contemplating learning to knit. "Hi."

"Kate."

"Yes."

"Oh, Kate." He felt better, hearing her voice. Or maybe he just felt safer, reminded of her existence by the soft warmth of her voice.

"Oh, Jack." She sounded almost tearful.

"Anything wrong? More dreams?"

"No, no—nothing wrong," she said quickly. "Everything's fine." There was a silence.

"So, how's the weather been over there?"

"Beautiful. The whole day was beautiful. And you?"

"I'm beautiful, too, but it's raining back here. I miss you, come back, all is forgiven, I'll even iron my own shirts."

"You always did before I met you," was Kate's dry comment.

"Well, I've developed this arthritis thing—"

"Run out already, have you?"

"I spill a lot. And then there's all the crying..."

"I left six clean, ironed shirts in the bottom drawer of my bureau."

"You didn't."

"No, I didn't."

"You didn't?"

Her laughter hadn't changed. "Go and find out for yourself after I hang up. Are you eating?"

"You sound like Tos. I did my own dinner in the microwave. Have you ever tasted chicken noodle ice cream?"

"You're breaking my heart. I had an old-fashioned English tea this afternoon—anchovy toast, potted shrimps, scotch eggs, scones just dripping with butter and strawberry jam, Eccles cakes, congress tarts, walnut gateau—"

"What the hell's an Eccles cake?"

"I'll bring you some home."

"You mean you'll bring some home with you."

"That's what I said, isn't it?"

"Not quite. You're turning English before my very ears."

"I'm not!" She sounded quite offended.

"Have it your own way. How's Richard?"

She didn't answer immediately, and, when she did, her voice sounded rather thin. Perhaps it was a bad connection. "Richard Cotterell I suppose you mean?"

"I suppose I do, yes. Did he have this vast tea, too?"

"You sound like a policeman."

"I *am* a policeman, remember? A dirty copper, see?" His Cagney imitation was never very good, and long distance did not improve it.

"Yes, he had tea, too. How's your investigation going?"

"It's not, it's just hanging there. Sniggering to itself."

"And little Miss Firefly from Washington?" On this subject, her voice was definitely thinner—despite the high-calorie tea party.

"Back in Washington—she had to check out some things. Returning tomorrow."

"Oh."

"Katie—" His voice was suddenly soft.

"What?" She was very far away.

"Nothing. What's on your agenda tomorrow?"

"Oh…more Shakespeare, of course. I'm giving my paper in the afternoon. I'm pretty nervous about it." There was a low mutter in the background. A male mutter. Unmistakably and clearly male.

"Who was that?"

"Just somebody talking. How did your court appearance go yesterday?"

"Fine. Talking to who?"

"To whom. To me. Apparently they're waiting downstairs. Some of us have been invited to an after-theatre party with some people from the RSC. It's a fantastic chance to meet some of the actors and the direc—"

"Downstairs? You mean you're phoning from your room?"

"Yes, of course."

There was a thirty-second silence. She was in her room, it was after eleven at night over there, and she wasn't alone.

"Jack? Are you there?"

"The timer just went off, Kate, I have to go, I have an angel food cake in the oven. Good luck with your speech tomorrow, I'll be thinking of you. 'Bye."

It is a scientific fact that the remains of a chicken noodle casserole, when smashed from head height onto a linoleum floor, scatters an average distance of six feet, and tends to go mainly under the refrigerator.

HE WAS STILL ON HIS KNEES, clearing up the result of his temper, when the phone rang again. Muttering, he went to answer it, trailing paper towels.

"Yes?"

"It's Dana. I have something, I think."

"Great. When will you be back?"

"I am back. I just got in."

"Oh."

"Did I get you out of bed? I'm sorry."

"No, no, I was just cleaning up a few dishes."

"Your turn in the kitchen?"

"My week in the kitchen—Kate's at a conference in England."

"Oh, I see." There was a pause. "Well, I suppose this could wait until morning, but if you feel like coming over to the hotel for a drink, I'd love some company."

"Is it that good?"

"The bar?"

"Whatever you got in Washington."

"Well—it's confusing," she said slowly.

He waited, but she didn't volunteer any more information. A little song began to run through his head. Everybody knows this game, it went, everybody plays this game sometimes, everybody loves this game—do you? Does Kate? Does Richard Bloody Cotterell?

"Give me half an hour," he said.

TEN

"JESUS! WE'VE GOT a correlation!"

The others stared at him.

"Guess who Hawthorne partnered during his three months on the job?" Pinsky demanded.

"Chief Franconi?"

"No. Phil Yentall."

Having leapt up at Pinsky's triumphal announcement, they now all sank down and stared at one another. Tos finally spoke.

"What does it mean?"

Pinsky, flushed with running up from Records, wiped his face with his handkerchief and stuffed it back into his pocket. A sudden and unexpected warm front had suffused Grantham from the south, and windows had been throw open to welcome the spring. How long the spring would last was anyone's guess. Maybe even until that night.

"It doesn't *mean* anything at the moment," Stryker decided. "Thanks to Dana, we know that Hawthorne grew up in Grantham and that for three months he was a member of the Grantham police."

"And now we know he served those three months partnering Phil Yentall," Tos said. "Hey, wait a minute. His prints must have been on our files, for crying out loud. Why the hell didn't we match them before? Why did they have to go all the way to Washington?"

"Because some klutz marked them 'inactive' and they haven't been transferred to the computer yet,"

Pinsky said. "They said they've been trying to get around to it, but with new stuff coming in all the time..."

"Oh, for crying out sideways," Tos said with disgust.

"Do you think knowing about Hawthorne would have saved Yentall?" Neilson asked.

Stryker considered it. "It might have made him more careful, because we'd have got to him about Hawthorne."

"Do you suppose it had something to do with this Higley man?" Dana asked hesitantly. "Maybe it was something about that, some secret between them."

Stryker sighed. "I've got someone trying to track Higley down, but it looks as if he left the city years ago. We can certainly have the phone records for Yentall's station and home checked out to see if he made any calls to Chicago. If he used a pay phone somewhere we'll never get it, of course."

"Why would he have called Hawthorne, anyway?" Neilson asked.

"I have no idea," Stryker said. "There was a gap of several days between Hawthorne's death and Yentall's, though." He got up and started pacing between his desk and the windows—following a path already clearly defined on the green linoleum, which was wearing thin in several places around the room. "Maybe Hawthorne called Yentall instead of the other way around."

"Why?" Dana asked. "Why would he?"

"Old friend, ex-partner, working cop, Yentall would have been the best one to give him current street information about the city. French Street wasn't in his precinct, but there isn't a cop in the city who doesn't know it, one way or another." He thrust his fingers through his hair, and rubbed it until it stood on end. Like the linoleum, it was going thinner, no doubt due to constant abrasion. "There was something Yentall's captain said—what the hell was it?" He stared at the far wall, and then his face cleared. "Right—I meant to ask him about it then, but I let it go. He said Yentall hadn't been sleeping too well lately."

"Do you think it was because of Hawthorne?" Dana asked.

"Could be."

"Hey, never mind the damned fingerprints. Why didn't *he* identify Hawthorne?" Pinsky asked suddenly. "His photograph was circulated. Yentall would have seen it for sure. Why didn't he come forwards?"

"Maybe he was going to," Stryker said. "Maybe that's why he got killed."

"Sure, I remember Gabriel Hawthorne," said Mrs. Yentall. They were seated in a glass-walled room at the side of the house, obviously intended more for use in the summer. The furniture was mostly wicker and there were bright flower patterns on the cushions and upholstery. The warm day had made it attractive and comfortable, and sitting there allowed Mrs. Yentall to keep her eye on the children in the yard. While she spoke, her eyes were always going to the windows and what was going on outside. It was like talking to someone watching television. "I remember him because Phil said he had the right name—always going around blowing his own horn."

"That sounds like Gabe, all right," Dana said, half to herself.

"They didn't get along?" Stryker asked.

Mrs. Yentall shrugged. She was a nice-looking woman, who probably fretted over her weight and shouldn't have, because the slight plumpness became her. But grief had dulled her skin and tightened her mouth, and there were dark circles under her once bright eyes. "They got on all right, I suppose. It was a long time ago, and they weren't together long. I remember they didn't part too happy, though. Hawthorne had this habit—if things went great it was him that did it, if things went bad, it was Phil's fault. There were others wouldn't have put up with him but Phil—" She faltered, then controlled herself. "Phil was easygoing. Always gave the benefit, you know?"

"I hear Phil was very popular with his fellow officers," Stryker said gently. "Captain Corsa said how much he was liked."

"He was. Hawthorne wasn't. He had a knock-down, drag-out fight in the locker room with some other rookie—"

"Colin Higley. Yes, we know about that."

"Higley went at him for letting Phil take the can for the Eberhardt mess-up. Nobody held him back, either. But they both had to resign. Phil felt bad about Higley, spoke up for him, but there was nothing he could do. Nobody listened." She looked out of the window. Two small boys were playing in the backyard, and as she looked, one slipped and fell into a particularly luscious mud puddle, sending muddy water flying over his brother. It was obvious the two of them found it hilarious, and gave every indication of doing it again.

"Good thing mud washes off," Stryker said.

Mrs. Yentall gave him a rather sardonic glance. "Not all of it does," she said. "Some sticks."

"Meaning?"

She sighed. "The Eberhardt case," she said patiently. "Like I said before."

"Oh. Right. How exactly was Phil in on that?" Stryker tried to remember what he'd read of Yentall's working history.

"He was the original arresting officer," she said. "Him and that Gabe Hawthorne caught the Eberhardt kid trying to rob a gas station, and took him in. But Hawthorne didn't Mirandise the kid and his lawyer got him off. Like I said—it all ended up looking like Phil's fault because he was the senior officer of the two, but he said he had told Hawthorne to do it."

"He should have done it himself, to make sure," Stryker said gently. "Twice doesn't hurt."

"Do *you* always do it twice, just in case your partner messed up?" demanded Mrs. Yentall. "Or do you trust him?"

Stryker nodded. "You're right. Sorry. But Eberhardt went to jail."

"Oh sure, he went to jail. For thirty days on possession of an offensive weapon—that knife of his. And look what happened. Everybody seemed to remember that it was Phil let him get away with it."

"Oh, I'm sure that's not true."

"Then how come he passed his sergeant's exams four *years* before he got promotion?" Mrs. Yentall said shrilly. "Always he got passed over, always they took someone else, never Phil. Even then, he made excuses for the department. It's the way the system works, May, he'd tell me. You got to be patient. You got to understand the pressures. He never got bitter, but me, *I* got bitter. He should have been a lieutenant, like you, maybe even a captain one day.

Now...now..." Her voice broke and she looked down at her clenched fists. A burst of shouting and laughter from outside drew her attention, and she stood up. "I got to get those kids in out of the mud," she said. "Do we have to go on any more?"

"No, that's all for now, Mrs. Yentall. Thanks for seeing us," Dana said, standing up, too. Reluctantly, Stryker rose to stand beside her.

Outside, walking down the path to the car he turned to her. "I had more questions," he said angrily. "I had more I wanted to know."

Dana shook her head. "You wouldn't have gotten your answers," she said. "Not right now, anyway. She's still too raw, hurting too much. And especially resenting the department too much. She'd keep retreating behind the children, the way she did just then. Believe me, it wouldn't have been any good. Maybe in a day or two, you could try again. Or someone else could."

"Look, she might have known something—"

"Fine, go back," Dana said, her own temper rising. "I work for the Justice Department, right? I've had to question a lot of people who have reasons to hate and resent the police. Chicago, Detroit, Milwaukee, New York—and women whose husbands have been killed hate their departments worst of all. Later, when they have a little time, it gets easier for them. They can stand the memories. But not now, Jack. Really—it wouldn't do any good."

He took in some of the warm spring air, drawing it down deep, and then let it go again. "Okay, we'll leave it."

They walked toward the car. "Who was Eberhardt?" she asked, as he unlocked the doors.

"A very nasty piece of work, liked to cut people up with his hunting knife," he said. "Tos and I put him away three years ago. How about some lunch?"

"Fine," she said, getting into the car.

He closed the door and then came around to slide behind the wheel. He sat there staring out of the windscreen but made no move to start the engine. "What did you have against Hawthorne by the way?" he asked carefully.

"It's personal."

"Is that why you were sent to liaise on this case?"

"Could be. My superior in the department has quite a sense of humour."

"Hawthorne doesn't sound like he had a winning personality."

She was staring straight ahead. "On the contrary, that's exactly what he had. Winning was all he cared about. Scoring and winning was Gabe Hawthorne's hobby."

"And?"

"And that's it. My guess is, if they find anything in the phone records at all, it will be that Gabe called Yentall. And if he called him, it wasn't for old times' sake—it was to use him. Gabe was a user. He had no doubt he was going to be right on top one day—and there would be a lot of footprints on a lot of faces to show how he'd got there."

"Sounds like you really hated him."

She glanced sideways at him. "You have good hearing."

He started the engine. "Let's get some lunch," was all he said.

ELEVEN

It was Pinsky's turn in court on the Bronkowsky case, so it was Tos and Neilson who went to interview the late Merrilee Trask's partner, Steve Chin. He was a handsome, compactly built Chinese American, with a very ready grin. His teeth were white and even, but there was one gold one in the corner of his mouth that always seemed to catch the light.

"Man, she was one tough mama," he said. "Scared the shit out of *me* more than once. That's for sure. It was like having your own private squad of marines. You know? I couldn't believe it when they told me she was down. Must have taken six guys, I said. Or a tank. But no. Just one shot. Right?"

"Right," Neilson said, mesmerized by the rhythmic appearance, disappearance, and reappearance of the gold tooth as Chin spoke, grinned and spoke again.

"We've been through her records. Do you think there might be any old cons that carried a grudge against her?"

"No particular one comes to mind," Chin said. "You think it might be someone with an old grudge that's shooting these officers down in cold blood?"

"We don't know," Tos admitted. "We're looking into every possibility. How about her personal life? Anybody there?"

Her ex-partner considered this. "She was a divor-cée, down on men, but she wasn't a lesbian or any-thing like that."

"You sure?" Neilson asked.

An odd expression crossed Chin's face. "I'm sure," he said.

"Boyfriends?"

"No—she said she never wanted to get emotionally involved with anyone again. She was lonely, I guess—but she put everything into the job. She was studying hard for her sergeant's exams—the job was her whole life, you know?"

"For all the good it did her," Tos said gruffly.

Chin shook his head. "I still can't believe she's not going to suddenly walk in here and yell for me to get my ass out to the car, she's ready to roll. They tell me I still flinch when a woman shouts in the hall." The quick grin came and went. "Don't get me wrong—she was a real great girl, and I liked her a lot. I felt terri-ble when they told me what had happened to her, still do. I'll never have another partner like her again, that's for sure." He had a strange look in his eyes. "Probably live longer, too."

"She took chances?" Neilson asked.

"Chances? She took *charge,* man. I mean I was senior officer by six months, but that didn't make no never mind to her, she knew it all, she did it all."

"And you didn't object?"

Chin grinned. "She was a lot bigger than me."

"Oh come on," Tos said impatiently.

Shrugging, Chin tipped his chair back and put his feet up on his desk. Around them the room was full of movement, noise, confusion, but Chin was calm and almost too quiet now. "Okay, okay—fact is, she made us both look good, you know? I'm not a very aggressive type, and she made up for it. I was grateful to her, in a way. Our arrest record was tops in the precinct lots of times, we got a couple of commendations—''

"You got a couple of reprimands, too," Neilson put in.

"Yeah, well—" For the first time, Chin looked uncomfortable, his air of overcheerful confidence slid away and he looked suddenly smaller. "She had a tendency, you know? She was what you might call too enthusiastic."

"You mean she used to beat the shit out of suspects now and again," Neilson said in a flat voice. "Like you lost a few convictions here and there."

Tos raised an eyebrow. "And it was *her* who did it?"

"Yes," Chin said in a flat voice. "I told you she was tough, and she was. Karate, mostly. And a short fuse. She never said, but I think her husband divorced her because she beat him up."

"She ever beat you up?" Neilson asked half jokingly.

"Not so it would show," the small man said, his skin darkening slightly.

Neilson gazed at him for a long time. "You're saying she knocked you around?" he finally asked in a disbelieving voice.

"You heard me," Chin said, the flush going even darker.

"But why would she do that?"

Chin looked down at the floor. "She had high standards," he said quietly. "She expected a lot, on and off duty."

"You saw her off duty?"

Chin looked away, picked up a pencil, inspected it, turned it around and around, dug the point into his blotter until it broke, threw it away. "Sometimes."

A brief silence hung between the three of them. Tos looked blank, but there was a dawning comprehension in Neilson's eyes. He didn't know whether to laugh or cry. The poor bastard, he thought. "I don't think we want to go into this," Neilson said finally.

"No, I don't think you do," Chin agreed in a sad voice.

"You sure you didn't shoot her yourself?"

Chin sighed. "I thought about it."

"What stopped you?"

"Nobody would have believed I objected," Chin said sadly. "I told you, she was a good-looking woman. To most people, anyway."

"Jesus," Neilson breathed. He got the feeling that Chin was relieved to have told someone—however obliquely—of this rather unusual form of police "brutality." Chin was right—there would have been plenty of cops who would have thought he'd lucked on to a good thing. And Neilson might have been one of them, if he hadn't been sensitive enough to feel Chin's pain from three or four feet away. There were all kinds of humiliation.

"You weren't with her when she was shot," Tos said, not quite certain he was getting any of this right. He'd have to ask Neilson about it later, he decided.

"No—I was taking some personal time," Chin said. "An errand I had to do for the family. Someone called in an abandoned car or something, and it was on her way to where she was meeting me for lunch. She never got there, though. To lunch, I mean. When I called up the station—they told me she'd been shot. That she was dead."

"How's your arrest record been, since she went down?" Neilson asked.

Chin smiled wryly. There was a person sitting there now, not a man in a grinning mask. "Lousy, thank you. But I can live with that."

"And you've got a new partner?" Tos asked.

"Yeah. Officer Linda Tang. That's her over there." He nodded his head towards a small Chinese-American girl who was standing by the coffee machine chatting to another woman officer. Officer Tang was petite, pretty, and had a delightful smile. "We're going undercover in Chinatown next week, cooperating with an FBI investigation of the Triads," Chin continued. "We're posing as a young married couple with money problems."

Neilson grinned. "Now she's definitely a good thing."

Chin shook his head. "She won't let me get near her," he said ruefully. He looked up at Neilson, sensing his sympathy. "Do you understand women?"

"I'm still at the research stage," Neilson said.

When they got back to the car, Toscarelli asked Neilson if he had understood the situation correctly—that Officer Merrilee Trask had sexually harassed her partner, forced him to sleep with her, in exchange for taking the lead in their street performance?

"That's how I read it," Neilson said, starting the engine and looking in the mirror to check for oncoming traffic.

"Why didn't I ever get a partner like that?" Tos wondered, thinking back to the photograph of Officer Trask, a full-lipped blonde with huge blue eyes. "How come you get Pinsky and I get Stryker and a timid little guy like that ends up with a luscious sex-starved divorcée?"

"We were just lucky, I guess," Neilson said.

TWELVE

THEY DROVE ABOUT A MILE and parked. He came around and opened her door for her, and they left the sunshine to enter a cool and quiet darkness. The restaurant was a small one, but they found a booth near the back. It was apparently not a "police special" for there were no uniforms among the customers, nor did any of them look like off-duty detectives. For some reason this encouraged her—it felt private here.

"I'm sorry I interrupted your interrogation," Dana said, when they'd started lunch.

He shrugged, and concentrated on his salad. "You were probably right. It's done now."

She watched him cutting up the cold chicken and detected a certain savagery. "You don't like me, do you?" Dana asked.

Startled, Stryker looked up and raised an eyebrow. "Wow, you sure like everything up front, don't you?" he said.

"That doesn't answer my question."

He poked his salad around the plate, hoping to discover another piece of chicken hidden under the herbage. "Most cops would resent federal interference on a local case."

"I'm not interfering. At least, I'm trying not to, but—"

"But when you see people messing up, you can't resist the opportunity to put them right."

"Like with Mrs. Yentall?"

"Like with everything. Whenever I do or say anything you get this superior look on your face, and I can feel your disapproval boring through the back of my neck."

"If you can see the look on my face, how come I can see through the back of your neck?" she asked, amused.

He stared at her for a minute, then threw his fork down. "Okay, very clever, you win again." He looked around the room to see if he could spot the waitress and get a beer.

"I wasn't trying to win," she said quietly. "I was trying to point out that you are being unreasonable."

"Am I?"

"Yes, you are."

He shrugged. "Okay, I'm unreasonable. This *case* is unreasonable, dammit. Officers going down right, left, and centre, we've got no leads, no connections, no—"

"One connection—Gabe Hawthorne and Phil Yentall and the man that killed them both. That's why I'm here in the first place, remember?" Dana looked across the table at him, and felt a tremor go through her. She was always talking about being open and honest—why not now? "But that's not why I'm getting under your skin, is it?"

"I don't know. Let's just drop it, okay?"

"The problem is called sexual antagonism," she said earnestly. "The sexual tension between us is causing a lot of problems. We really should resolve it."

He stared at her. "Jesus—you are something else, you know that?" Stryker said, shocked as much by her frankness as by the instant realisation within himself that she was absolutely right. He'd wanted to screw her from the minute she'd walked into his office. If only to shut her up.

"It's true, though, isn't it?"

"I would imagine very few men would find the prospect of going to bed with you repellent," he said. "I just don't happen to be the kind of guy who—"

"Don't be pompous," she said. "I'm only trying to clarify the situation."

"The situation is simple—I'm in love with someone else," he said stiffly.

"I see."

"Tell me—do you always work like this?" he asked. "Are you one of those new women the magazines talk about—just straight out with it, wham, bam, how about it?"

"No, I'm not. And I'm not saying 'how about it,' necessarily. But working together would be so much easier if we could just get our motivations out in the open—"

"I don't *want* my motivations out in the open," he snapped. His voice dropped with every word, until he was speaking in a savage whisper. "I don't want this kind of hassle, I don't want complications, I don't want to go to bed with you."

"Liar. I want you and you want me. That doesn't mean we have to *do* anything about it, but it's there, all the same. It's nothing to be ashamed of, you know." She found she was whispering, too, and wondered why. They couldn't be overheard.

"Thanks for the compliment—but all I want is to solve this case, okay? That's all I want." He was still desperately searching for the waitress. Or a waiter. Or a plumber. Or an architect. *Anybody*.

Dana leaned back in the booth and regarded him coolly. "That wasn't all you wanted at the hotel last night. I saw it in your eyes. I could feel it all the way across the room the minute you walked in. But you didn't follow through. Why?" She still burned with the memory of going up to her room alone, as turned on as she had ever been in her life, and as frustrated. They had talked about the case for an hour or more, and then he had left, saying he needed to sleep on the information she had brought from Washington. Didn't the man realise the effect he had on women? Or was it just on her?

He glared at her. "What you felt was anger and jealousy, that's all. I'd had an argument with Kate on the telephone and when you called I just—felt like getting out of the house." He flushed, looked down at his plate, at his hands clenched into fists on either side of it. Slowly he opened them. "Maybe you're right. Yes, okay, you're right. It was all there, you and the night and the music, the hotel room upstairs, the whole bit on a platter. You looked beautiful, exciting, and I wanted you. But—I couldn't do it. Wouldn't do it. Not for those reasons. I hope I'm never angry enough to hurt Kate like that."

"I see." Dana felt a little shocked at herself—but exhilarated, too. As if she'd done something very dangerous, and survived. "Your Kate must be quite a woman."

"She is. She could give you lessons on being a woman." He hadn't meant it as unkindly as it came out.

"I don't want lessons on being a woman," she flared. "I was a woman for years and I didn't like it. Women get stepped on, pushed around, and hurt.

They're always being hurt. That's why I decided to play with the men instead. It's much easier that way."

"Is it? You don't seem very happy about it."

"Why should I be happy? I just got told I'm not worth the risk."

Stryker nodded. "That's right—you're not. But don't you see? Nobody is, as far as Kate and I are concerned. Despite my dashing good looks and swashbuckling manner, I am actually a pretty square guy. Do you turn me on? Yes, you turn me on. Do I *want* to be turned on by you? No, I do not. So I get angry. I'm sorry. I have other things to do. And I have enough risks in my life as it is. I think you should think about risks, too. Men get rejected by women all the time. If you want to play from the men's bench, you'll just have to accept the same results. Win a few, lose a few. If this sexual antagonism stuff is going to keep us at each other's throats, so be it. You're right, it's good to know about it, but now that we *do* know about it, can we forget the goddamn stuff? Can we get back to doing what we're supposed to be doing and at least try to be civil to one another?"

"I didn't think men like you still existed," Dana said in a distant voice.

"Yeah, we exist," he said wryly. "We call ourselves the Dumb Clucks Brigade. Maybe it's love, maybe it's laziness, who knows? But we turn down beautiful women all the time. Beat them off with sticks and staves, shouting 'Fidelity, fidelity.' It's very exhausting, very hard on the nerves. Are you coming back to work, or are there several men in the restaurant you'd like to proposition, first?"

To the amazement of them both, tears sprang to her eyes. "That was unfair," she said. "I'm not like that. I've never been like that."

He regarded her gravely. "Then I'm sorry," he said, after a minute. And meant it. His voice was quiet and a little sad. "From the way you were talking, I thought I was just another one of those things with you."

She grabbed her handbag and slid out of the booth. "So did I, damn you," she said, and hurried towards the exit.

BACK AT HEADQUARTERS, Tos and Neilson told Stryker about their interview with Steve Chin. "Merrilee Trask was completely different from the other victims," Tos said. "It makes things worse instead of better. I'm down to wondering if they all belonged to some secret organisation or something. Maybe they were all members of some cult."

"Anything to indicate that in other interviews?" Stryker asked.

"No," Neilson said, shaking his head. "Like Tos says, they were all completely different types. Randolph was an idealist, Santosa was an insecure rookie, Trask was a gung-ho eager beaver, Yentall was easygoing, and Hawthorne was a one-man band. They didn't seem to have anything in common as far as their performance evaluations went, and they seem to have even less in common in their private lives and personalities. I say it has to be random. What else could it be?"

"I don't know," Stryker said helplessly. "Jesus, I just don't know."

"Why not accept that it's random and go from there?"

"Because there's nowhere *to* go from there," Stryker said. "I think we just keep working on every possibility we can turn up until something snaps into place. Who's handling the psycho files, again?" He looked very harassed, and his hair was already standing on end as he ran his hands through it.

"Jake Chase and Joe Kaminsky." Even as Tos spoke, there was a crash in the outer office. "There they are now."

Stryker went to the door and looked out, then opened it and spoke wearily. "Were those the psycho files?"

A tall, dark man looked up from where he was kneeling between the desks. "I wasn't anywhere near them," he said in a resigned voice.

"You don't have to be," Stryker said. Chase was fated to be the centre of disasters. Small and large—if there was a problem, he was bound to be in the middle of it. Sometimes, however, that proved a very advantageous place to be, as his record of successes proved. "Have you come up with any possibles, yet?"

"One or two," Chase said, standing up with both hands full of papers. "Come to think of it, make that twenty or thirty. Joe and Stan Feltzer are still checking them out. I had to take Casey to the doctor's this morning. Looks like I'm going to be a father."

"Accident?" Stryker grinned.

Chase shook his head. "No—but a surprise. I didn't even know I was pregnant."

"Give Casey my congratulations. And Jake—" Chase looked up from sorting the files. "Get someone else to hold the baby during the christening."

"You bet," Jake laughed.

Stryker closed the door and waited for the next crash. When it didn't come, he started back to his desk, whereupon there was a sound of rending fabric. He didn't turn around, just raised an eyebrow at Tos, who stood up slightly to look through the glass door.

"Captain Klotzman's dress uniform, just back from the dry cleaners," Tos said. "It was hanging—"

"Spare me," Stryker said. He stood and thought, then turned to Neilson. "Okay—if Ned is still in court, then you and Dana go down to City Hall and see what you can dig up on the ownership and backing of the French Street mission."

"Great," Neilson enthused, looking at Dana and nodding. "We'll find it, whatever it is, right?"

"Sure," she said in a dull voice. He glanced at her in surprise, but she didn't meet his eyes. "I have all the Washington listings in my briefcase—all we need to find is one name—a person or a company or anything—and it will give us an edge we can start to peel back."

"Good." He kept watching her, wondering what was wrong. She had been silent ever since she and Stryker had returned, staring out of the window and taking no part in the conversation. He could feel the tension in her clear across the room. "What do you think it is?" Neilson asked Stryker. He tore his eyes from Dana. "I mean, what do you think the connection is?"

"I'm still not convinced that there *is* a connection." Stryker was walking around the office again, back and forth, back and forth, but never near the window, where Dana stood looking out at the building opposite, an extremely dull edifice that offered no visual stimulation whatsoever. She seemed to find it fascinating. "I think Hawthorne was killed for some other reason altogether, but until we figure out what it is, we might as well pursue Dana's line. Okay?"

"Okay by me." Neilson was delighted with the prospect of an afternoon in Dana Marchant's company. As he recalled, Municipal Records was housed in long, dark corridors and small, isolated rooms. Who knows, who knows? he thought to himself, watching her. This could be Harvey Neilson's lucky day. She was beautiful, she was single, and something had obviously gotten under her skin. Whatever it was, he had the afternoon to make it better. He knew a dozen ways.

Stryker turned to Tos, who had been watching him closely. "Problem?"

"No," Tos said, raising his hand in mock defense. "No problem here. How about you?"

"I'm fine, for crying out loud. I'd be even better if you'd stop staring at me. What makes you think there's anything wrong with me? I even ate a salad for lunch—happy?"

"Thrilled," Tos said drily.

"Okay, you and me, we go down to French Street again. Rivera is down there, and he might have something for us."

"Fine."

Stryker turned to Neilson. "Did Ned say how long he thought he'd be in court?"

Neilson shook his head. "Nope. He says he sat there all morning, but they got tied up with other witnesses—something about Bronkowsky's drug connections—and now they might not even get to him this afternoon, but he has to hang around just in case."

"Who's Bronkowsky?" Dana asked.

"One of the big boys here in Grantham," Stryker said. "Has his fingers in a lot of pies, and what he doesn't like he spits out. His last rejected item was a set of twins named Clancy who had been on his payroll, but accepted an outside assignment—to bump off Bronkowsky himself."

"Who gave them the assignment?" she asked.

"Nobody knows for sure, since they're now very dead themselves and not saying much. Guesses range from his wife, who has been playing around but hates to let go of his money, to a couple of up-and-coming rivals who would very much like to take over some of his business interests. Bronkowsky is a very rich man."

"Taxes?"

"They tried—he has some good fronts and some even better accountants. No, they have to get him on this one, and the DA is working hard. Trouble is, he's a little strapped for evidence, thanks to a dirty cop named Leary who knows the answers but has to be kept off the stand."

"But if he knows the answers—"

"He knows a lot of other stuff, too," Tos put in. "Stuff that would louse up this particular case but good—as well as opening up several cans of worms the department would like to keep sealed and on the shelf. He threatens to spill it *all* if he's called—and if he's called, the defense attorney will give him every opportunity to do just that, in order to take the attention of the jury off his client."

"Why doesn't the defense attorney just call him?"

"Because the DA subpoenaed him for the prosecution. You can't do both sides."

"He could call him as a hostile witness."

"That would give the DA a chance to cross-examine him on the Clancy killing. I think it's called a Mexican standoff. So he goes to court and sits there—but nobody says a word to him."

"But that's—"

"Expedient," Stryker said repressively. "We like to clean up our own messes without benefit of media. Maybe they do things differently in Washington."

"That's where the art was perfected," Dana said. "We have canned worms, too."

Stryker started to put on his leather jacket, then thought better of it and threw it over his chair, choosing instead the soft tweed that Kate had bought him for Christmas. It would remind him of her every time he looked down. He thought being reminded of Kate would be a good idea at the moment. He wondered what she was doing—which was definitely *not* a good idea. Damn all Englishmen, anyway. "Was Leary in court?" he asked Neilson.

"Ned said he left about halfway through the morning. I don't know why the bastard sits there day after day, he knows he's never going to get called. Ned said things lightened up considerably once he went out."

"The spectre at the feast," Stryker said, reaching for his old tweed cap and pulling it down over his eyes.

"Hey—you're under arrest!" Neilson said. Stryker scowled at him, and Neilson gave him a dumb grin. "That's the kind of cap the killer wears," he said.

"My cap is only guilty of dandruff," Stryker said. "Anything else is purely coincidental. Coming?"

Tos arose from his chair and joined Stryker. "What kind of salad?" he asked the smaller man, as they went out the door. "What else did you have?"

Neilson looked over at Dana. "It's a nice day and about a ten-minute walk to City Hall. Or would you rather drive?"

She dragged her eyes away from the fascinating blank face of the building opposite and looked at him. He was clean and neat and very attractive in his way. He was probably a bastard, though—they all were, weren't they? Did it matter? Probably not.

"Let's walk," she said. "You can tell me your life story on the way."

Neilson was startled, but game. "You got it," he grinned.

THIRTEEN

"THERE HE IS."

"That's not him."

"Yes, it is."

"Oh, come on—" Tos squinted at the shabby figure lurching along French Street, with its torn overcoat flapping around its ankles, matted filthy hair, and several days' growth of beard. Under the coat were several ragged sweaters and a pair of enormous trousers held up with a length of clothesline. "That's not Mike Rivera. I *know* Mike Rivera. I partnered him for six months just after we got out of training."

The pathetic figure turned and made a filthy gesture at their car as they passed, shouting an obscenity after them. Stryker drove on for about a block, then turned into an alley and cut the engine. "It is," he said.

"Never."

After a few minutes the shabby figure appeared beside Tos's door and rapped on the window. Tos rolled it down and then pulled back as the figure leered in at him showing blackened teeth and exuding a strong odour of cheap gin. "Hiya, wop," the figure said.

"My God," Toscarelli said. "You little spic bastard—that's a hell of an outfit."

"My mother knitted it for me," Rivera grinned.

Tos grinned back. "She does good work."

Stryker leaned forwards to peer around his partner's bulk. "How's it going, Mike? Got anything for us?"

"I think maybe. It's nothing definite yet, but I got a feeling about this Cot place. Some of the people there are not so bad off as they make out, you know? Their dirt doesn't go much deeper than mine does. I think the place is being used for something, but I haven't cracked it yet. I have to get closer in. I'm a new face, they're being careful, maybe a day or two more. Maybe a week, if it's something they're really protecting. You know? Takes time."

"We leave it to you," Stryker said. "But if you come up with anything, get it to us pronto, yeah? Especially if it's anything connected with something called Abiding Light."

"Yeah, yeah, I got all that," Mike said impatiently. "I'm working on it, okay?" He glanced up the alley and then suddenly fell backwards against a dumpster. "Hey—what the hell! Leave me alone!"

Stryker glanced in the mirror. "Friends coming—make it quick."

In a flash Toscarelli had the door opened and was out, grabbing a fistful of Rivera's filthy coat and shaking him like a dog shakes a rat. "You scummy little bastard!" he shouted into Rivera's face. "Next time be careful who you mouth off to, right? You understand me? You got that?"

"Lay off! Lay off!"

Down at the mouth of the alley several disreputable characters had joined the first man, who had taken three steps into the alley, seen the car and Rivera, and had stopped to stare. "I got a mind to teach you a lesson, you piece of shit!" Tos yelled.

"Leamme, leamme alone!" Rivera squealed. "I done nothin', I din' mean nothin', leamme go!"

"Son of a bitching little scumbag!" Tos yelled, and with a sweep of his hand he knocked Rivera up and over the edge of the dumpster. There was a thud as Rivera's well-padded figure hit bottom inside. "That's where you belong!" He made a show of dusting his hands, then turned towards the mouth of the alley. "Anybody else got any smart remarks about my mother?" He made a menacing step towards them, and they scattered. "Bums!" he bellowed after them.

He turned back and started to get into the car. "You all right in there, Rivera?" he asked, sotto voce.

Rivera's voice reverberated dismally within the metallic confines of the dumpster. "Yeah. Wonderful."

Tos chuckled, and got into the car. Stryker gunned the engine. They sped out of the alley and turned with a squeal of tyres towards a better neighbourhood.

"How is it that Mike works this thing of his?" Tos asked. "Nobody seems to know the details. And how come we got him on this?" Tos asked.

"We haven't, exactly," Stryker said. "We just sort of got added to his list. He's been down here on and off for the past six months, undercover, working up a character. Some new approach they're letting him develop. He comes, he goes, the others get used to him being around, and they open up. He's dropped some pretty good stuff in—more reliable than using snitches because he knows how to ask and how to listen. It's on a year's trial. At the moment he's trying to 'dry out' at the Cot."

"Must play hell with his home life," Tos reflected.

"I hear he hasn't got one anymore. His wife divorced him after their boy got killed. I'm not sure

whether she blamed him or the department or what—
she was a cop, too, she should have known as well as
anyone how these things happen. Mike coped with it,
she didn't. She left, he stayed on—and I guess she
couldn't stand that. Anyway, since then Rivera has put
everything into the job. Real gung ho, I hear. His loss,
our gain."

"Sort of like Merrilee Trask," Tos said. "Except I
presume he hasn't been beating people up."

"The reverse, from the look of him. I hope he
thinks it's worth it."

"Would you?" Tos asked.

Stryker thought about it. "I don't think so. I'm not
that dedicated.

"Not since Kate came along, you mean?" Tos asked
slyly.

"I guess so."

They drove on a few blocks in silence. Tos glanced
sideways at his friend and partner, then ventured to
speak again. "That Dana is really something, isn't
she?"

"You, too?"

"Sure, why not? I'm human, I'm normal, I'm
available."

"I thought you and Liz Olson had a thing going."

"Off and on, sure, but I haven't signed the pledge
or bought the ring or anything. Not like you."

Stryker kept his eyes on the road, slowed for a stop
sign, then drove on. "What's that supposed to
mean?"

Tos shrugged over-casually. "Anybody can be
tempted."

"Not everybody gives in to it."

"Sure. And not everybody gets so goddamn crabby about it."

Stryker clenched his jaw. "Observant bastard, aren't you?"

"I am a professional detective of some years' experience," Tos said smugly. "Also I know you like a brother. You and Kate are having problems, right? That's why you didn't go to England with her."

"She doesn't want to marry a cop."

"Who does?"

"Other cops—sometimes."

"Isn't any better that way—Rivera's wife was a cop, wasn't she? That didn't work. Butterfield married a cop, Schuster married a cop, they all busted up. It's not the kind of job you have, it's the kind of person you are. Or aren't."

"I like you better when you stick to telling me what I should eat," Stryker said. "When you get married or set up house with someone, *then* I'll listen to your advice to the lovelorn."

"I'm also available for consultation on interior decoration, travel, investments, and the removal of warts," Tos said.

"I need some coffee," Stryker said. "Call in a break for us, will you? What about the Robin Hood on Greenfield?"

"Okay—I like their bran muffins. They use those big raisins in them," Tos said, reaching for the radio to notify their destination to Despatch.

THE BRAN MUFFINS were apparently up to scratch, for Tos ate four, scowling at Stryker's choice of a cinnamon jelly doughnut, but saying nothing about it aloud. They said very little, in fact, but sat avoiding one another's eyes, absorbed in their individual thoughts, taking stock. A pause in the day's occupation.

When they emerged into the parking lot at the side of the restaurant, there was a slight chill in the breeze, and clouds had built up from the north. It looked like spring would be a little short this year. Toscarelli went around to the passenger side and got in, but Stryker stood beside his open door, gazing up at the sky.

The first shot was low.

It caught him in the left shoulder, throwing him against the door. The hinges protested, but their metallic groan was lost in his shout of pain.

"What the hell, Jack?" asked Toscarelli from inside the car, because he hadn't heard the distant report, and only saw Stryker lose his balance as he cried out.

Then he saw the blood.

"Jesus!" He reached for the radio handset. The second bullet shattered the rear window but never made it to the windshield.

Toscarelli's head deflected it.

Stryker, who was sliding down the door and clutching his shoulder, saw the impact—saw the flying chips of bone and the blood. He screamed "No!" in rage and protest as Tos was flung forwards against the dash and then fell back on the seat, his face unrecognizable under the flooding mask of blood.

There were no more shots.

"Tos . . . Tos . . ." He called to his partner, but saw nothing, heard nothing that said warmth, breath, life. He lifted himself from the ground and worked his way across the seat under the steering wheel, reaching out with the hand that still worked, feeling the blood sliding down the one that hung uselessly by his side. It tickled as it ran between the hairs of his arm. It didn't seem right that it should tickle when everything else was hurting. He touched Tos, briefly, then found the coiled plastic lead, followed it, and pulled the handset from under his partner's motionless body. He pressed the button to transmit.

"Code 9—officer down. Robin Hood Grill, Greenfield Road near Telegraph. Code 9, Code 9," he said into the microphone. There was a crackle, a tinny voice from the speaker underneath the dashboard, a sound of questions he was having trouble understanding. He was in between a rock and a hard place, between shock and pain, between anger and despair, and things were difficult there. He drew a breath, fighting the pain, and screamed into the handset.

"Officer down!"

Someone was choking, someone was sobbing, and he hoped it wasn't him but he had a terrible feeling it was because he couldn't see Tos very well now. It was as if he were watching television, and the picture was bad, kept wavering, kept threatening to disappear altogether. The big man was just lying there, with the blood pouring down his face and dripping off his nose and chin—already there was a big puddle on the floor. The blood just kept on coming, the puddle was just getting bigger and bigger, and nobody was doing anything about it. It was a disgrace. Somebody should do something about it. He pressed the button on the handset again.

"Code 9—officer down," he whispered. "Please..."

FOURTEEN

"I THINK I HAVE SOMETHING," Dana said.

"Lady, you have everything, as far as I'm concerned," Harvey Neilson said, gazing dreamily at her. "Let's give this another twenty minutes and then break for about two weeks. I was thinking Hawaii."

"And here I was thinking you were a police officer," Dana said. "I guess you're just on an apprenticeship or something, is that it?"

"I'd like to learn a lot about you."

Dana sighed and turned away from the microfilm screen to glare at Neilson for a change. "How old are you?"

"Twenty-eight and in my prime," Neilson said, lifting his chin in case he was showing any puppy fat.

"You must watch a lot of television."

"Hardly ever touch the stuff," he protested.

"Then why does your conversation sound like old Warner Brothers scripts?" Dana asked. "You're too young to have seen them in Saturday matinees."

"I had other things to do during Saturday matinees," Neilson said expansively.

"Oh, God—the spitball king of row G, were you?"

"Not exactly." He was irritated at her lack of respect. Also he felt peculiar—she wasn't giving the right responses. Usually when he made his play for a woman, he either got slapped in the face or accepted. This smart-ass stuff was tiring, and definitely not worth it. "Look, sorry if my conversation bores you—"

Dana turned back to the screen. "I didn't say it bored me, exactly—"

"Well, then—" He brightened.

"But this is not the place for it."

"Name the place, just name it." He leaned a little closer. There was no one around, and while this cold basement room was not exactly his choice of venue first time out, she—

"328 Porter Avenue."

Neilson straightened abruptly. "Where the hell is that?"

"It's the address of the Abiding Light Association in Washington. And it's the same address given here for Boston Footwear, owned in turn by Cardinal Enterprises, who hold the lease of the French Street Mission, here in Grantham. We've got our connection, Harvey! Now we have to find out who owns Cardinal. That would be under C—"

"Congratulations are in order," he said, and taking hold of her swivel chair he turned her around and kissed her, thoroughly. When he had finished, he looked at her and smiled, broadly, waiting for compliments.

She stood up. "I think the C section is one row over," she said, and disappeared back into the stacks.

"Damn," Harvey muttered. Well, that was it. He'd given it his best shot and failed. Okay, fair enough. There wasn't much point in trying anymore. She was frigid, that was it. Definitely a frigid girl. The trouble was, he couldn't make that fit with the definite impression he had that under all that tough exterior there were fires burning. He also had the feeling she was fragile, and easy to break. It worried him. It also worried him that it worried him—because he never bothered to think that much about the women he went after. Mostly they were girls he met in singles bars, or got introduced to at parties. They were bed or non-bed. You hoped any effort you put in to get them into bed was worth it, but if not, better luck next time, right, Harvey, boy?

But this one worried him. This one was different.

He found her leaning against the shelves, eyes closed. "Hey," he said, concerned. Maybe she was sick, maybe that was why she didn't respond to his kiss. "You okay?"

She opened her eyes and looked at him. "Delayed reaction?"

"Oh, right—I forgot I put that in," he said modestly. He looked at her more closely. "Are you sure that's all it is?" he asked. "I mean, I know I'm devastating, but—"

"Can I level with you, Harvey Neilson?" she interrupted.

He looked alarmed. No girl ever levelled with him. Not Good-Time Harvey, Laughs and Jokes a Specialty. "Sure," he said, cautiously.

"I am thirty-four years old. Does that bother you?"

"Only in the nicest way," he said. "I like older women." That didn't sound quite right. "Not that you're exactly—"

She ignored him and went on. She seemed to need to make things very, very clear. That was good, Harvey thought, because I don't know what the hell is going on here.

"I have recently suffered a rejection," Dana said. She really did sound like Miss Johnson. "I am feeling vulnerable, and in need of reassurance. However, I am from out of town and not interested in a long-term relationship. You have a certain animal attraction. Also, I like your after-shave. We could have dinner tonight and discuss all of this, or we could just let it go. Your decision."

He stared at her. Brains, that was it, she was one of those brainy women, right? Maybe she was laughing at him. She didn't *look* as if she was laughing at him, though. She looked like she was just saying the truth. She also looked like a teacher he used to have a crush on in the tenth grade, Miss Johnson, beautiful and unreachable. He would have died for a chance to hear Miss Johnson make him this offer. He couldn't refuse. Harvey was in trouble, and he knew it. Trouble right up to his goddamn eyebrows. "I always get hungry around eight," he said, rather unsteadily.

"Fine. Now, can we look for Cardinal, please?"

"Who rejected you?" He would punch the bastard out.

"It doesn't matter." She moved away, running a finger along the files.

"I guess I should be grateful to him, huh?"

Dana turned and regarded him. "No, I should be grateful. Are you a bastard, Harvey?"

"No!" He was hurt.

"I meant are you a stinker, a rogue, a rat with women?"

Now he was suspicious. "Who's been talking about me?"

"Are you?"

"Maybe a little bit," he conceded. She was really throwing him off balance. What the hell was the matter with her? "Hey, listen, I don't pretend to be *perfect,* but I never make any promises, so—"

"That's good," Dana said. "That's fine. You're just what I deserve." She went back to the files.

"I think I've just been insulted," he said, after some consideration. "I think maybe we should forget the dinner."

"Whatever you say." She didn't seem to be upset about it one way or the other. Harvey felt a wave of miff wash over him. He had never encountered this kind of situation before. Dealing with women was easy, everybody knew how to do it. You lied, they lied, everybody lied, it was easy. It was The Game. Wasn't it?

"Well, what do you mean, anyway, you 'deserve' me?" he demanded.

She lifted her lovely shoulders. "You're going to hurt me," she said negligently. "You're going to break my heart."

"I am not!" He'd never broken a heart in his life. Some said it was because he didn't have one himself, but that wasn't true. He had one—he just never let it out on its own, that's all.

She turned her big smoky eyes on him, and he felt his kneecaps start to go. "Oh, yes, you are. And I think I'll be glad. Do you understand? It will mean I've let myself out of jail—become a woman again. Does that make any sense to you?"

"Not a goddamn bit," he said bitterly. "Dinner is definitely off."

"Okay." She shrugged and turned back to the shelves. She moved along them, then spoke again, carelessly. "Who's that big, good-looking blond detective whose desk is over in the corner of the outer office at headquarters?" she asked. "I think his name is Eddie or—"

"Oh, hey, listen, now—he *would* hurt you," Neilson said quickly. "Eddie Klusky is a real son of a bitch with women; you want to stay away from him. If you're determined to get 'hurt' like you're saying, you better do it with me. You can trust me."

She turned to look at him. He looked at her.

She started to laugh.

"You never laughed before," he said.

"I know," she agreed.

"You look funny when you laugh," he said, badly shaken now. "Like a little girl. Your nose wrinkles up—"

"I know," she said, and laughed harder.

He stared at her in a kind of wonder. The more perplexed he looked, the more she laughed. He began to laugh, too, although he didn't know why the hell he was doing it because this girl was definitely crazy and he would be smart to drop the whole thing but he couldn't. He couldn't. They both jumped at the sound of a clearing throat.

"Excuse me, is one of you Officer Neilson?"

"Me, I'm Neilson. I think," Harvey said in a strangled voice.

"There's a telephone call for you at the desk. I believe it's urgent. Something about your union?"

Neilson, thoroughly unsettled, stared at her. "The Police Federation is calling me? *Here?*"

The clerk looked apologetic. "Well, but they said something about a striker being shot. Maybe you'd better speak to him yourself." Neilson stared at her, then moved, fast, towards the phone. The clerk turned to look at Dana, who was staring after Neilson's retreating back, all traces of laughter gone from her white face.

"I didn't know the police were on strike," the clerk said. "Did you?"

FIFTEEN

THEY WOULDN'T LET HIM SIT up until the X rays were back.

"Look, I can wiggle my fingers, for crying out loud!" he kept protesting, but they just smiled and said rest, now.

The overhead light was in his eyes, making them water, and he kept wiping it away with his good hand. He asked one of the doctors to turn the light out. They couldn't, so they moved the table he was on back a little, but it didn't help.

The tears kept coming.

Pinsky appeared and stood beside him.

"Did you get the bastard?" Stryker demanded, knowing the answer already because he knew Pinsky and could read his eyes. "Goddammit!" he said, as Pinsky shook his head. "And Tos?"

Pinsky opened his mouth, closed it, opened it again. His voice was rough and he cleared his throat. "They're operating on him now."

"He's not dead."

"No, he's not dead." The word that hung in the air, almost visible in that very bright, very painful light, was "yet." Pinsky swallowed. "The bullet took some skull and some brain, but they said it wasn't important brain, whatever that means."

"It mean nonfunctional matter," put in the intern who was keeping an eye on Stryker while waiting for the X rays to come back. "We've got a lot of extra stuff up there in the skull just hanging around. He might be lucky. Which side was it?''

Stryker raised his good hand and sketched the path of the bullet as he remembered it. The intern nodded.

"He might be lucky," he repeated in a doubtful tone, and straightened up from where he had been leaning against the wall. "I'll see what's holding up those X rays." He went out, and the cheerful flowered curtain flapped shut behind him. Stryker looked at Pinsky.

"You looked for him?"

"We're still looking," Pinsky said. "We've got people going over that street with nit combs. Harvey's still there."

"That's good—Neilson is a fussy son of a bitch."

"Yeah, Dana's outside."

"Keep her there." He shifted slightly. They'd given him something to dull the pain in his shoulder. They didn't have anything for the rest of it. "We'd checked with Rivera on French Street, then stopped for coffee. We're getting into the car when bam! comes the shots, from nowhere. Rifle, wasn't it? Had to be, there was nobody in sight." He'd answered his own question. "Filthy goddamn bastard . . ."

"All right, all right, take it easy," Pinsky said.

"Which one of us was he after?"

"Does it matter? He got you both," Pinsky said grimly.

Stryker clenched his left fist, almost enjoying the wave of dull pain that surged out and down from his injured shoulder. "*Why,* for Christ's sake?"

"If we knew why, we'd probably know who," Pinsky said, trying to be reasonable. It was an effort, with Stryker lying there and Tos up in surgery. Jamming his hands in his pockets, he went over and inspected the stainless steel trolley that held the suture packs and quite a lot of Stryker's blood on gauze and cotton balls. In a kidney dish was the bullet they'd taken out of Stryker's shoulder. "Looks like a 7.6."

"Felt like it, too," Stryker agreed, trying to turn his head to look. It hurt to pivot on his ear and he gave it up, addressing the rest of his remarks to the overhead light which was still giving him glare. "You'd better take it."

"I guess." Pinsky felt in his pockets and eventually produced a small brown envelope that had held his electricity bill. Using a piece of gauze, he carefully picked up the bloodied bullet and inserted it into one corner of the envelope, then tucked the packet in his inside jacket pocket. "We dug the one that hit Tos out of the dashboard—too distorted to read anything from it. This one looks better."

"So glad to be of help," Stryker said bleakly.

The intern came back, looking cheerful. "Missed the bone."

"Told you," grumbled Stryker. "Can I go now?"

"We'd like to keep you for obs—"

"Hell with that. I'm a cop. I've been shot before. I want out, I'll sign whatever you want."

"Jack, maybe—" Pinsky began.

"No, I want out. I want to get to work."

The intern sighed. "There's dedication and there's dumb." He met Stryker's glare and gave in. "Okay, okay, I'll strap you up. You won't be able to get much use out of that arm for a week or so. And remember you've lost a lot of blood, so you'll feel weak for a couple of days."

"I've lost blood before," Stryker said.

"Oh right—I forgot, you're a big, tough cop. So you know about shock, too."

Stryker stared up at the light, and watched again the long, terrible moment when Tos was hit and thrown against the dashboard and then fell onto the seat and his good Italian blood was everywhere. Everywhere. "Yeah—I know about shock," he agreed.

HE LEANED HIS HEAD BACK against the wall in the waiting room, having chosen a straight chair as the one least likely to let him fall asleep. Dana was beside him, as pale as he was, too shocked to speak, for which he was inordinately grateful. She was just a pretty girl now, and nothing more. Shock insulated him from anything else; it was a shield and he was grateful for it. He wondered, weakly, whether this was retribution for his even having considered—what he had considered. He couldn't even form it in his mind, except that it had to do with betrayal and Kate. Pinsky was in the corner of the sofa opposite, pretending to read a magazine. They all looked up every time there was a flicker of white past the doorway.

Dana felt totally isolated. These men were accustomed to sudden violence, but she was not. Although outwardly she might appear to be as calm as they, it was not calm but a numbness she had only once before encountered—when Peter died. She had to seem calm and brave for little Pete, but then as now it was a frozen kind of calm that she felt did her little credit. No praise was due for being a zombie because she hadn't willed it—it had simply arrived and taken her over. She walked, she talked, she functioned—it meant nothing.

When somebody finally came in, it was Neilson.

"How is he?" he demanded.

"We're waiting," Pinsky said.

"I'm fine, thank you," Stryker said.

Neilson turned to look at him. "Yeah, I know *you're* fine, I asked downstairs already. You look like hell."

Stryker shrugged and instantly regretted it. Neilson winced sympathetically. "Oops—that was a mistake, right?"

"Right," Stryker agreed. "Did you find anything?"

Neilson's attempt at being cheerful faded. He sat down on Dana's other side, but did not touch her, instead leaning forwards with his elbows on his knees, and rubbed his face. "Not a goddamn thing, unless you count about fifty used condoms and two thousand beer tins." He unbuttoned his jacket and leaned back. "We found where he fired from, though. Or we think we did. Upstairs in a derelict building. Marks on the windowsills, footsteps in the dust. The forensic guys are in seventh heaven, crawling around in the cobwebs, talking to the spiders, bribing the rats for a description. Of course, rats don't rat on rats, do they? I forgot."

"Cartridge cases?"

"Picked 'em up. He did, I mean—not us."

Pinsky tossed his magazine back onto the table in the centre of the room. "Really?"

Neilson shrugged. "We found where they fell, sure. But they weren't there, and they hadn't rolled. Believe me, we looked."

"That's very interesting," Dana said. "Somebody who knew what was dangerous to leave around, and took the time to pick it up."

"Somebody who likes to kill cops," Neilson said in a strangled voice. "Jesus, I want that bastard."

The others stared at him. "You think it's the same one?" Pinsky asked. "I haven't even given the bullet to Ballistics yet."

"I can smell it," Neilson said.

"But how did he know we were cops?" Stryker wanted to know.

"How did he know Yentall was a cop?" Neilson countered.

"Yentall was parked in a police lot," Stryker pointed out.

"Yeah—and you were parked next to a restaurant used a lot by cops. The car wasn't a black and white, but it sure as hell was a department car. He could have spotted the radio. All he had to do was stake it out and wait for you to come back to it." Neilson's anger was difficult to contain, but it was not really directed at Stryker.

Stryker sighed. "Okay, okay," he conceded wearily.

"Getting shot has slowed him down some, I see," Neilson commented.

"He'll catch up," Pinsky replied, and picked up another magazine.

A doctor appeared, looking young enough to still be in high school, and tired enough to have been on his feet since birth. "Sergeant Pinsky?" Pinsky nodded. "Sergeant Toscarelli is out of surgery and in intensive care. The damage was less than we thought—he has a good chance of complete recovery."

"Thank you," Pinsky said. "Thanks very much."

"*De nada,*" the young doctor said. "Maybe you can see him tomorrow, depending."

"Depending on what?" Neilson wanted to know.

"On what kind of a night he has," the doctor said. He turned to go, but stopped at the croak of Stryker's voice.

"You said the damage was less than you thought."

"Yes."

"But there was damage?"

"Oh yes."

"What kind of damage?"

The young doctor leaned against the doorjamb. "That area of the brain covers motor controls, mostly. Until he's conscious, we won't know what has been impaired and what has been saved. At best, he could have a full return of faculties."

"And at worst?"

"Possible paralysis to a greater or lesser degree, difficulties in speech, that sort of thing. As I say, we have to wait until he can tell us or show us. We hope for the best, though." With a quick and unconvincing smile, he was gone.

Stryker found his sight going again.

Pinsky stood up. "Come on," he said to Stryker. "I'll take you home."

"I don't know what the hell's the matter with me," Stryker said wiping his face.

"It's shock," Pinsky said kindly. "Blood loss. You feel weak, you know? You got to expect that."

"Yeah," Neilson agreed, taking Stryker's jacket from Dana and carefully arranging it over his sling. He looked away while Stryker tried to press the tears back into his eyes. "Shock and stuff. Happens all the time."

"Not to me," Stryker snapped. "Goddammit, not to *me!*"

SIXTEEN

"I GUESS I'D FORGOTTEN what it was like," Dana said slowly, as she and Neilson drove away from the hospital. "Working at a desk in Washington the way I do is pretty far removed from the street." She looked down and saw that there was blood on her skirt. It must have come from Stryker's clothing or bandage, but she couldn't remember being that close to him.

He hadn't let her get close to him.

"Keep her out of there," he'd said to Pinsky in the Emergency Room. His voice had been weak, but it had carried far enough to slap her in the face. She didn't for a minute think it had been to protect her from the sight of blood. It had been to protect himself from what he assumed might be an emotional display.

Well, she was stronger than that, and he should have known it. The fact that her knees had nearly buckled when they'd brought him out from behind the curtain—his face white and pinched and angry—was irrelevant. It had been very hot in there, and she had never liked the smell of hospitals.

It reminded her of Peter, and of all those months when the smell of hospital had gone home with her every night and penetrated every empty room in their apartment. She could never speak about it, about anything concerning that terrible, terrible year when her husband had died. No matter how tightly she had held his cold, thin hands, Peter had slid away from her inch by inch, like someone disappearing under the ice into black water.

Gone forever.

"Hey," Neilson said, suddenly noticing the glisten of tears on her face. "It's okay, they're going to make it." He regarded her quizzically. "The question is, are we?"

"I don't think so," Dana said. "Not tonight."

"Terrific," Neilson said. He was surprised to feel relief. The fact was, his original enthusiasm had been considerably dimmed by the afternoon's events, but to admit it would be to seriously damage his reputation with himself as a ravenous sexual beast. "So, do I drop you at your hotel, or what?"

"Yes, fine—the hotel would be fine."

They pulled up in front of the hotel, and he left the engine running. "Ah—this thing with us," he began awkwardly. "Maybe we should let it go?"

"Do you want to let it go?"

"Hell, no—I was just giving you an out, right?" He leaned forwards to look into her face. "I mean, you seem pretty upset and all about Jack getting shot—"

"It's not that, exactly. What you see here beside you is a woman beginning to . . . um . . . emerge."

"Like a butterfly coming out of a cocoon, hey?" He thought she might laugh, but she didn't.

"You said I could trust you," she said.

He frowned. "Yeah, well—up to a *point* you can trust me. I'm not a bum, but on the other hand, I'm no angel, either. I told you, I never make promises or—"

"I want you to understand," she said. And so she told him all about Peter and hospitals and Gabe Hawthorne and all the empty years she'd filled in with the cement of pretending not to care. She even told him how Stryker had made her realise what she was doing to herself. It poured out like infection from an old wound, cleansing her and transfixing him. Harvey listened in dismay—he was unaccustomed to hearing confession—and throughout her speech he smiled at her blankly, wishing he could think of something to say or do that would make it all right.

When she came to a stop, all he could think of was, "You'd better get some sleep." He knew it was inadequate—he suddenly felt inadequate all over.

With a sigh, she said goodnight and got out. He watched her enter the hotel. Her looks were somewhat diminished by fatigue, but she still turned heads. She certainly had turned his—he felt quite dizzy.

This whole thing was getting too heavy for him, he decided. He liked to keep things light, he liked his world to be casual, simple—and here she was, treating him like a deep-thinking person or something. He didn't want to hurt her, nobody halfway decent would want to hurt her, but on the other hand, he didn't think he was—he stopped himself just before he got to "good enough for her."

What kind of a thing was that for Absolutely Wonderful Harvey Neilson to be thinking?

"Hell with that noise," he said aloud, and revving the engine into a defiant snarl, he pulled away from in front of the hotel with a screech of tyres.

He picked up a pizza and a six-pack on his way home, slumped in front of the television to watch an old John Wayne movie, and wondered why he didn't feel like cheering the Duke as usual.

Damned woman.

THE ROOM WAS DARK, except for the television set flickering soundlessly in the corner of the built-in bookshelves that flanked the fireplace. Stryker lay on the couch with one of Kate's patchwork quilts over him, and the cat on top of that. He scratched behind the cat's ears and grimaced as on the screen he saw the top of his own head disappearing through the emergency entrance of the hospital, the rest of him hidden by paramedics carrying his stretcher. Just before him Tos had been taken in under an ominously stained blanket.

The six o'clock news had just finished, and he was watching the weather report without benefit of commentary. During the report on the lunchtime shooting, his heart had practically turned over when he realised that the blanket was over Tos's face—was he dead and they had all been lying to him? Then a corner of the blanket had flipped back momentarily, and he saw Tos's hand lying on the stretcher. Saw it move, saw the fingers twitch, and realised the blanket coverup had been to protect the onlookers, not Tos.

The weathergirl looked inordinately cheerful, despite the fact that she seemed to be drawing all kinds of black clouds and depressions on the maps. He closed his eyes for a minute.

He jumped when the telephone rang on the table behind the couch. The cat, with a reproachful glance, retreated to the foot of the couch and began to wash as Stryker reached over and picked up the receiver.

"Hello?"

"Hi."

"Kate? Aren't you supposed to be giving your paper?"

"I finished hours ago, silly. It went very well."

"Great. Good girl. I knew you'd dazzle them."

"Oh, sure, you know me."

He was so glad to hear her voice he nearly burst into tears again, and mentally cursed his weakness. "What's next on the busy agenda, then?"

"We just finished dinner. I expect I'll be going to bed when the talking runs down." She sounded both excited and exhausted.

"Aren't you supposed to be in there with your mouth hanging open at their display of wit and erudition?"

"Nobody will miss me. I was—"

"Not even Richard?"

She sighed. "I wish you'd stop going on about Richard. I *knew* you got the wrong idea about his being in my room. He'd just called in to see if I was ready to go down, that's all."

"What a gentleman."

"There are a few left in the world."

"Excluding cops, presumably."

"No, including cops. Jack—what's wrong?"

"What do you mean?"

"While I was eating dinner, I got the most terrible feeling that something was wrong. That's why I called."

"I thought it was only bad dreams you had. Now it's waking whim-whams, too? You'd better see someone abo—"

"Jack—there *is* something wrong, isn't there?" She'd heard it in his voice, then. Maybe he'd been trying too hard.

"Well—sort of. Tos got shot—but he's going to be okay."

"Shot?" Down the wire her voice became shrill with sudden panic. "Are *you* all right?"

"Hey, hey—I'm fine," he lied. "I'm here at home, talking to you—it's Tos who's in the hospital, right?" Well, that was the truth. "I'm fine." That wasn't the truth, but he was better than dead.

"Where was he shot?"

"On Greenfield Road."

"No, no... where in the body?"

He sighed. "In the head—but it's okay, Kate," he said over her moan of horror. "It took away a bit of bone but it was really just a deep crease. Nothing vital hit. Eyes, nose, teeth, all present and accounted for. Ears as well. Really."

"You're hurt, too. I can hear it in your voice. I'm coming home first thing in the morning."

"Don't be ridiculous. I'm just worried about him, that's all. They say he'll be okay, but I won't be happy until he wakes up and begins telling me off for not eating my greens or something. You know how he's always fussing about my health, like a goddamn Jewish mother. So now I'm returning the favour."

"I don't believe you."

He wanted like hell for her to be there. "You want me to be shot? Okay, I'm lying here in a cast from neck to ankle, blood dripping from every pore, screaming in agony every third minute. Your only consolation is that while I'm in this plaster overcoat I can't chase women. Or at least, not as fast as usual."

"I see." She was wavering.

"I'll hire an ambulance so I can meet you at the airport. Don't forget to bring me some Yorkshire pudding and some Scottish shortbread. What time will you be getting in?"

There was a long pause, and he could hear her thinking. He almost hoped he hadn't convinced her, because he could conceive of nothing nicer at the moment than her cool hand on his fevered brow and maybe being read to, like a kid with measles. She finally spoke.

"Who shot him? Was it—was it that cop killer?"

So he'd teased her out of worrying about him. Why did he feel so disappointed? "We don't know yet. It was from quite a distance away, so it was a rifle. They're checking out the marks now."

"It could be the same person."

"You and Neilson ought to get together."

"He thinks it's the same one?"

"Yeah."

She sighed. "So I had a premonition about Tos."

"You mean you're starting to worry about him now, too?"

"I've *always* worried about him, too," she said.

"Yeah, I know," he said softly. "Sorry."

There was a pause—and then he heard her take a deep breath. "I'm coming home."

"No."

"But I've *given* my paper—"

"*No!* Forget it. We're all grown-ups here, we can look after ourselves," he said, more sharply than he'd intended.

"I can't help worrying," she snapped back.

"Neither can I—but it won't make a goddamn bit of difference whether you're worried over there or back here."

"Well, thanks a lot—so nice to know I'm needed."

"I didn't mean that. I meant—"

"I know what you meant."

There was a silence. They both seemed to realise simultaneously that they were on the verge of an expensive transatlantic argument, for as he opened his mouth, she spoke quickly, overriding him. "Well, I guess I can go back to this terribly important conference. Since you're okay and all that. You are okay, aren't you?"

"Nothing a night's sleep won't improve." He was being so careful choosing his words, you'd think he was Richard Bloody Cotterell.

"I'm sorry about Tos."

"Me too. But it will be okay, I've still got Neilson and Pinsky."

"And Miss Fireplug," she reminded him. "Or should it be Mrs.?" Oh, such an innocent little voice.

"She's a widow."

"Oh. Shame." Ah, but there was no pity there.

"She can help out a little more, until Tos is back on his feet. Why not? Anyway, this is costing a fortune. See you in a week," he said briskly.

"Only three days now."

"In three days, right. No more premonitions, okay?"

"I'll notify my subconscious immediately." She could be brisk, too. The phone clicked down. The connection was broken.

He hung up the phone with a sense of guilt about the evasions. When she came home in three days and found him with a hole in his shoulder, she would raise hell.

Well, so what?

In three days he would have his strength back.

If he was lucky.

He didn't feel very lucky.

KATE PUT THE PHONE BACK on its hook and stood there, staring unseeingly at the dial. Slowly she turned and walked to the nearest chair. Around her the lobby of the hotel was fairly deserted—those attending the conference were still in the dining room, enjoying after-dinner brandy and bullshit. She'd had enough of both. All day long, Stratford had been full of visitors. The lush spring sun had brought them to marvel at the daffodils and crocuses that swathed and spangled the grass along the Avon. All during the long morning and afternoon of talk after talk, her attention had wandered to the windows. On the pavement outside, crowds of people passed, the clatter and shuffle of their footsteps audible through the open casements. Children shouted, and there was laughter. It seemed as if everyone was hurrying to some kind of parade or celebration, but it was only the hysteria engendered in the English by sudden warmth and brightness. They were unaccustomed to it; it went to their heads.

Kate wished it would go to hers again. She felt suddenly suffocated by the soft lighting and rich surroundings of the hotel lobby, stood up, and fled into the cool night air. The novelty of being able to walk the night streets buoyed her up for some blocks, and then she began to feel chilled. She felt a moment of alarm when she heard the footsteps behind her, but then she heard Richard's voice.

"You must be wishing you'd brought a coat," he said quietly, and draped his dinner jacket over her shoulders as he drew level with her. She started to protest, then saw he was wearing his raincoat.

"Thanks. I think I was about to get lost."

"That phone call upset you." It wasn't a question—he must have been watching her. That disturbed her momentarily, but she didn't know why.

"Yes. My—Jack's partner has been shot."

"Is that the one you call Tos?"

"Yes. He's in the hospital. Jack's not telling me everything, I know he isn't. I'm sure he's hurt, too. I feel it."

"But he was at home when you rang?"

"Yes," she admitted reluctantly.

"Well, then, if he *is* hurt, it can't be very bad, or they wouldn't have let him leave hospital."

She smiled wryly. "You don't know Jack. If he could walk they would have had to tie him to something to keep him there."

"There you are then. He can walk. How bad can it be? He's a grown man, he can look after himself for a few days."

"That's what he said."

"Sounds like a sensible chap," Richard said levelly.

"He's not, he's an idiot!" Kate snapped, on the verge of tears. "He's always trying to protect me, to pretend police work is safe—but someone tried to kill Tos. And Jack, too, I'll bet, only he won't admit it."

Their footsteps echoed off the closed shopfronts, her heels tic-tacking on the uneven paving stones. The warm day had given way to an evening of light mist, haloing the streetlamps and making the pavements glisten. Droplets of mist glistened in the dark curls of her hair and gave a dewy glow to her cheeks, which were flushed with frustration. "Well, from what you say, they didn't succeed. And if you had been there, nothing would be any different, would it?"

"No," Kate admitted reluctantly. "That's the whole trouble. I don't make any real difference to anything."

"I can't believe that. You would certainly make a difference to me and my life."

"No, I wouldn't—because your world and mine are the same. That's what I mean. Either I give in to Jack, or he gives in to me. I love the man, and he loves his work. How can I ask him to give it up? And yet, every time he goes out the door—" She raised her hands and then let them fall. "I die a little."

"Maybe you should end the relationship." Cotterell's voice was quiet. "Now that you're away from it, you can look at it more objectively, can't you? It sounds destructive to me. Your paper was superb, Kate. You obviously have a great academic career in front of you. What kind of work will you do if you're constantly fretting over this man of yours? Is it worth it?"

Kate stopped and stared at him. Richard stopped, too, and faced her, standing very close. He had loosened his collar, and as he raised an eyebrow his face took on a rakish, almost piratical cast. Handsome devil, they called him, and it was an appropriate description.

"Well?" he asked again. "Is it?"

SEVENTEEN

IN THE MORNING, Stryker thought he was going to die.

Being alone in the house and free to express the inner man, he let out a howl of pain when he first tried to sit up in bed. After that, only a steady, full-throated, and enthusiastic stream of curses sustained him through washing, getting into his underwear, and trying to make and eat breakfast one-armed. At the end of it he was totally exhausted, and Pinsky and Neilson had to finish dressing him when they arrived, around seven.

"They should have kept you in the hospital overnight, then you could have had a couple of good-looking nurses do this," Neilson said from where he knelt on the floor tying up Stryker's trainers. He screwed up his face. "They'd have been used to smells, too."

"They said Tos had a good night," Stryker said.

"I know—we called, too," Pinsky said.

"Did you tell Kate about it?" Pinsky asked. He and Neilson had been on the sidelines of the relationship from its beginning. Pinsky was a sentimental optimist. Neilson wasn't.

"I told her Tos was hit."

"Did you tell her how bad?" Neilson asked, standing up.

"I don't *know* how bad," Stryker said evasively.

"And you didn't tell her about you?"

"She'd have only gone bananas. By the time she comes back the worst will be over."

"So she isn't coming back right away?" Pinsky asked. Stryker could tell he was disappointed in her. "You're going to have to go on like this, by yourself?"

"Why not? It's no big deal," Stryker lied.

"Jesus—then tomorrow *you* tie his shoes," Neilson grimaced. "If I have to do it again, I'm putting in for hazardous duty pay."

"Let's go," said Pinsky, looking at his watch.

"How's the case going?" Stryker asked, over-casually.

"What case?" Pinsky asked.

"Those two guys yesterday," Stryker said. "Those two cops who got shot up, Stryker and Toscarelli."

"Oh, *that* case," Neilson said, pausing in the hall. "Investigations are proceeding. Do you want to wear your hat, or not?"

WHEN THEY WERE IN THE CAR and on the way to the hospital, Stryker took up the thread again. "So tell me about investigations proceeding," he said, wincing as Neilson hit another pothole.

"Which ones?" Pinsky said, lighting his pipe and waving the smoke into Neilson's face. Neilson was trying to give up smoking, and Pinsky had bet him twenty bucks he couldn't do it. Neilson growled at him. Pinsky grinned and puffed enthusiastically. "We've got an insurance scam, we've got a domestic killing out in the Hills, we've got two dumb cops got ambushed, we've got a hooker screaming justifiable homicide—"

"That one."

"The hooker? Sleazy Sal the—"

"No, the two dumb cops."

"You're supposed to lay back and let the big boys play with that one—Captain Klotzman's orders."

"Why?"

"You're a sick man." Neilson found another pothole. "See how much it hurts when I do that?"

"So don't do that."

"No sense of humour," Neilson said to Pinsky.

"Never had," Pinsky sympathised. "Your gems are wasted on a bad audience, Harve."

"Have you got any leads?" Stryker persisted from the backseat.

"Nice day, isn't it?" Pinsky said to Neilson.

"Supposed to rain later," Neilson said.

Stryker leaned forwards and took hold of Pinsky's collar. "Talk to me, you bastard, or I'll cut off your wind."

Pinsky broke free without much effort. "Knock it off, Jack. Klotzman said you were out of this one, and that's it."

"Why? Why out?"

"Because you're a victim, of course," Neilson said.

"Balls," Stryker said. "There's got to be more to it than that. Why is he down on me all of a sudden?"

"He's not down on you," Pinsky protested, straightening his tie. "But you're not the only cop in the shop."

"I'm the only one who got shot and is still on his feet." Stryker said. "If there is a connection, maybe I'm the best one to see it."

"You? Why?" Neilson swung into the hospital parking lot. "You think you're the only one with brains?"

"No," Stryker said evenly. "If this is part of the cop killings, and if the killings are random, then the odds against me getting hit again are about sixty zillion to one, so I must be one of the safest cops walking around, right?"

"Maybe," Pinsky said sourly.

"Alternatively, if the killings *aren't* random, if there *is* some connection between all the ones who have died, then there's a connection with Tos and me. A connection that's still there, and still alive, and still dangerous."

Neilson turned off the engine and both he and Pinsky turned to stare at Stryker. "You mean he might go after one or both of you again?" Neilson asked.

Stryker looked at Neilson approvingly—the boy was coming along. "Yeah, that's just what I mean. Which gives *me* a damn good reason for getting him first."

TOS WAS STILL UNCONSCIOUS.

He lay, large and still beneath the white sheet and blanket, his long eyelashes crescented on his pale cheek. His sideburns curled out rebelliously from beneath the white bandages that swathed his head, and his moustache drooped as usual over the corners of his mouth. There were tubes going in and out, something dripped continuously into him, and his chest rose and fell.

But Tos was not at home.

Beside his bed sat his mother and his sister, patiently watching his face. Mrs. Toscarelli, short, stout, and robust, greeted Stryker the way she always did—like a long-lost son returning from the wars. Perhaps she clung a little more tightly than usual—he did the same, although with one arm out of action it was a lopsided hug. When he had disentangled himself, he greeted Marina. It was difficult to see her as Tos's sister—where Tos was large and bearlike, Marina was as thin and soulful as an El Greco saint. In her late twenties and unmarried, she attended her widowed mother like an acolyte, despite the latter's enthusiastic efforts to find her a husband.

Mrs. Toscarelli nodded at Pinsky—he was married, after all—and smiled at Neilson, who was not.

"How is he?" Stryker asked, when the greetings were over.

"He sleeps," Mrs. Toscarelli said.

"Has he said anything?"

"No," Mrs. Toscarelli said, sitting down again and returning her gaze to her son's face. "He sleeps, we wait."

"We wait," echoed Marina in her moth voice.

Puzzled, they sought the doctor they had seen the day before and tried to get answers. There were none. Tos was alive and his vital signs were good, there was brain activity, his heartbeat was strong and regular, there was only slight fever which, considering the trauma to which he had been subjected, was an excellent indication that he was a fit and healthy man.

He just hadn't woken up yet.

But hadn't the anaesthesia worn off?

Oh yes.

Then why hadn't he opened his eyes, spoken, moved?

He wasn't ready to do that yet. They didn't know why. It was just a matter of waiting. Stryker said it first.

"Coma."

The young doctor sighed and nodded. "If you like, yes. He's in a coma."

"How long?" Stryker demanded.

"With head injuries it's impossible to tell. Ten minutes, ten hours, ten days—you figure it. We know very little about comatose states, really, other than the physical parameters. It may be simply nervous exhaustion. It may be a form of self-protection. A vacation from reality, if you like, while healing goes on."

"Vacation or escape?"

The doctor—whose name was Bishop—shrugged. "Take your pick. All we can do is look after him physically and wait. To interfere actively at this stage would be foolish—it could be only a matter of hours before he comes around of his own accord. We're keeping a close eye on him. Don't worry."

"I bet you tell that to all the boys," Neilson said.

EIGHTEEN

KLOTZMAN SHRUGGED. "Look, Jack—the way it looks now, you and Tos got unlucky, that's all. It was your turn—your number was up with this bastard." Klotzman leaned back in his chair, which creaked heavily. He was a short, broad man with acne scars on his sallow face, which was partly obscured by his heavy-rimmed glasses. He was fanatically neat, and spent as much time tidying his desk as he did actually working. He had a clear idea of a captain's duties and responsibilities, and was a stickler for detail and routine. All these faults were overlooked by his men, because he would fight for them all the way to the top and back again, and was scrupulously fair to everyone, whether he liked them or not.

Beyond the glass walls of the captain's office the work of Central Homicide went on quite smoothly without either of them. Men picked up apparently silent phones and mouthed into them, typewriters moved noiselessly, someone kicked the coffee machine and it drooled coffee without a sound—and without a plastic cup falling into place.

"Some nut, that's what I make it."

"Some nut with good aim and enough smarts to pick up his cartridge casings."

Klotzman waved a negligent hand. "Not good enough aim, this time, or you wouldn't be sitting here mouthing off at me. As for this cartridge case business, hell, everybody watches television these days. A

couple of episodes of 'Quincy' and they're all forensic experts, could do PMs on their kitchen table and
ballistics in the garage. Maybe he's a miser—or a litter fanatic. Who knows?''

"I know my partner is out for the count and I'm a
temporary one-armed paperhanger,'' Stryker said. "I
know we're cops and there's somebody out there
who's been killing cops for the last month. I want to
nail him.''

"I'm sure you do,'' Klotzman agreed. "All the
more reason for you not to work the case, Jack. I
don't like tempers in my cops, you know that. I like it
cool, quiet, steady—that's how to get the work done.''

"It's one way.''

"As far as I'm concerned, it's the only way,''
Klotzman sat forwards again, picked up a pen, drew
some papers towards himself. "Everybody in the department is full of rage over this; you're no excep-
tion. Cops are walking the street just aching for a
chance at this guy. We all want him, we all want our
hands around his goddamn throat, Jack. Jesus, how
we do. But when you're seeing red, you're not seeing
other stuff. An angry cop is an ineffective cop; he's
wearing blinkers, he's putting what *he* wants in front
of what's the intelligent thing to do. Maybe even in
front of what's the *legal* thing to do. And I don't want
that. I especially don't want it from you. You're moving up steadily in the department, Jack. You've got
everything it takes and there are people with their eye
on you for bigger things, believe me. But if you go off
half-cocked, maybe they'll start looking somewhere
else. Do you get my drift?''

"I don't give a damn about promotion.''

"And I don't give a damn about losing one of the best men I've ever had in my line? No way, Jack. Get off it. You take your sick days like a good boy. Maybe you should fly over to England, after all."

"And have Kate go berserk? No thanks. I'll just renew my library card and visit the art museum."

"Good idea," Klotzman murmured, head down.

Like hell, Stryker thought.

He went across the room to his own small office and sat in his chair, which also creaked, but at a much deeper pitch than Klotzman's. Neilson and Pinsky were already there.

"So?" Stryker demanded. "What are you going to do about it?"

Neilson and Pinsky exchanged a glance. "Just what we've been doing with all the rest," Pinsky said.

"Tell me about it."

"You *know* about it," Neilson said.

"Tell me anyway—I'm a sick man, I need humouring."

Neilson shrugged. "Okay. As far as you and Tos are concerned, same initial routine as with the others. First we go through all your old convictions and correlate them with recent prison releases. Plus any recent arrests released on bail. If we're going to relate it to the other killings, we enter as many relevant details as we can into the computer and run it against the profiles we have on the first four. And Hawthorne, too, I guess. Maybe this time it will spit something out—so far all it does is hum and smile foolishly at us. If it gives us zip, then we check again with Chase on the psycho files, plus the cop-haters file. If we come up empty after going through all that good stuff, we've got *real* problems, because our possibilities are all in-

visible—the ordinary citizens who've snapped under
recent pressure and nobody has noticed. Or the right-
at-the-edge obsessives who suddenly decide killing
cops would make a social point. Oh, I nearly forgot—there's also all the recent arrivals from all points
north, south, east and west who aren't on our files and
who bring their hates with them and maybe noticed
your name in the paper yesterday—''

''Was my name in the paper yesterday?''

''Yeah, twice—in a report about the Bronkowsky
trial, and in an article about the sniper. And this
morning you're all over it, of course. 'Latest victim'
and all that.''

''Fame at last.''

''And look what it got you,'' Neilson pointed out.

''You forgot what it will get us,'' Pinsky said.

''What?''

''All the new false confessors who will jump at this,
knowing the super-plus extra attention they'll get, both
from us and the media,'' Pinsky said. ''We'll have to
check all those out, as well. We haven't finished going through the ones who showed up for Yentall yet.''

''Inconsiderate bastard to hit again so soon,'' Stryker said sourly.

Neilson looked bleak. ''Do you suppose they have
any openings in Traffic? I feel one of my headaches
coming on.''

''How can you have one when you *are* one?'' Pinsky asked, unfolding upwards and heading for the
door.

Neilson put on a hurt expression as he followed him
out. ''That was unkind, Ned. That went deep. You've
upset me, now—really upset me.'' He winked and
waved good-bye to Stryker as he closed the door.

Through the glass Pinsky's reply was inaudible, but his grin said it all.

Stryker smiled wryly. It was almost like watching Tos and himself on a case. But Tos was lying white and still in the hospital, and he was sitting here on his ass, nowhere to go, nothing to do. He picked up his coffee mug and threw it into the corner, where it smashed loudly and completely.

Didn't help. Didn't help at all.

HE WAS STILL SITTING there three hours later. The spattered coffee had dried on the walls and floor, and the shards of the mug were lying where they had fallen. He'd had a call from Dana who was back searching the files at City Hall, and he'd made several calls of his own. Other than that, he hadn't moved.

Outside, it was nearly dark, and the lights of the city had begun to reflect off the low clouds that had swept in, bringing a soft spring rain. Stryker leaned forwards to turn on his desk light, and grunted with the pain that lanced through his shoulder. Sitting still for so long was rare for him, and his body reacted to it with some perplexity. A still, dark shape behind the pool of light, he was isolated in his glass-walled office, a silent fish lurking in the shadows of a busy aquarium. He watched the outer office slowly empty of one tour, and then fill up again with the next. Men going out greeted men coming in. Some lingered to exchange news over coffee, others simply waved and headed for an hour's unwinding over a beer before heading home to the other world they lived in—a world of wives and kids and, in some cases, understanding.

Any one of them could be the next victim.

Any one of them could catch the killer.

Either way, he could still be sitting here when they did.

The office door swung open and Neilson stood there.

"How about a lift home?" he asked.

Stryker sighed and levered himself out of his chair. He struggled into one arm of his coat, and Neilson helped him drape the other half over his shoulder. Neither of them said anything, either there in the office or on the way home. When Neilson pulled in to the curb in front of the house, he killed the engine.

"I'll get you settled," he said.

"Oh hell, I can manage," Stryker grumbled, but he was grateful for the company, and the protest ended there. They walked up the path and he handed his keys to Neilson, who unlocked the door and turned on the lights. "Thanks," Stryker said, and reached for the keys, but Neilson was already in, holding the door open for him.

"I think the phrase is, nice place you got here," Neilson said, looking around. "I'm impressed." He ran his eyes over the mixture of comfortable modern and antique furniture, the floor-to-ceiling bookcases on the far wall, the paintings on the near wall, the polished floorboards, the rough-woven curtains that complemented the big bright rag rugs.

"Thanks," Stryker said wearily. He started towards the kitchen. "How about a beer?"

Neilson looked at him with exasperation. "No, thanks. Listen, why the hell don't you stop with this goddamn strongman act and go lie down, for crying out loud? I'm really getting bored with this stiff upper lip crap."

"That should read stiff upper lip crap, Lieutenant, *sir,*" Stryker grinned.

"Uh-huh. Downtown you get 'sir,' here the best you can hope for is eye contact," Neilson said. "Sit down, I'll figure things out for myself after I've used your john."

Stryker sank onto the couch just as his legs began to shake. Neilson was right—kidding himself that a bullet wound couldn't slow him down made no more sense than pretending he wasn't going to go on investigating the case. Klotzman might say no, but he was going to *do* something. Anything.

Tomorrow.

Meanwhile, he was damn glad Neilson was here. Upstairs he could hear him moving around the bedrooms, then going down the hall to look out the back windows. He knew what he was doing. Checking things out. He nodded. Neilson was a bit of a smart ass, but his instincts were sound.

And he was fast.

After a few minutes, he heard the bathroom door close. He reached for the remote control and turned on the television, watched a cartoon for about thirty seconds, and then slid down onto the cushions and dozed off.

He woke up when the shotgun went off.

Jumping up from the couch in a blind panic, he took five steps and nearly tripped over Neilson who was lying on the floor and cursing.

"Son of a bitch, son of a bitch, son of a bitch."

The television set was dead.

The screen was in shards, the innards flashing and sparking. Shaking, his head still throbbing from the burst of sound, Stryker knelt beside Neilson. "Are you okay?"

Neilson rolled over and took hold of Stryker's arm, then wriggled with him back behind the safety of the sofa. "Of course I'm not okay," he muttered, peering around the end of it towards the kitchen door. "I go out to the kitchen to get us a beer and skid on that stupid rug. As I go down my hand hits the kitchen door, shoves it in, and a goddamn cannon goes off. My hair is singed, my suit is a mess, and my nerves are shot. Am I okay, he wants to know. Stay down, you stupid bastard!" he hissed as Stryker started backing up on his hands and knees around the far end of the sofa.

"I am staying down," Stryker said in a shaky voice. "What was it?"

"Sounded like artillery but probably a twelve gauge. Thing is, I don't know if one barrel went off or two. Maybe he's waiting with the other one." Seeing what Stryker was doing, he turned and started to crawl after him and get his gun out at the same time. As he wore it in the back of his trouser band, his progress was erratic. A single pellet of the charge had caught him high on the forehead, and a thin trickle of blood ran down into his left sideburn.

Stryker, gun drawn, stood up against the wall and with his back against it began to slide towards the kitchen door, the edge of which was scarring and smoking. It was an ordinary swing door, no glass. With his back flat against the wall beside it, he reached out and pushed the door in, slowly.

When it was about halfway in, the shotgun went off again.

"JESUS CHRIST ON A GODDAMN CRUTCH!" Neilson shouted, ducking behind a chair. "WHAT ARE YOU, CRAZY?"

Having now taken two blasts, the television set began to burn quietly to itself. The smell of melting electrical components blended with the smell of gunpowder, singed paint, and scared men.

"It was just one barrel that went off the first time," Stryker croaked, leaning against the wall. "Did you ever hear of a three-barrel shotgun?"

"No. But I have heard of guys who carry two guns. Forget it." Neilson was up now, and had edged along the wall to stand beside Stryker. "How about calling for help? How about begging for mercy? How about, in any case, getting the hell *out* of here?"

"There's nobody in there," Stryker said, with a notable lack of conviction.

"Do tell? Then, every time the door opens, who lets loose?"

"Every time the door opens, *it* lets loose. It's a setup, Harve."

"This is a theory of yours, is it?"

Stryker wiped his forehead with his good arm, nearly knocking Neilson in the eye with his .38. "Yeah."

"And you really feel confident about it?"

"If he's in there, he's taking a hell of a long time to follow through," Stryker pointed out. He felt rather short of breath.

"I, myself, am not big on theoretical police work." Neilson coughed. The smoke from the television set was filling the room. "Also I think maybe we are starting to burn the house down, over there, which your bank and your girlfriend are not going to like."

"She's been wanting an excuse to change the drapes," Stryker said. "How about across the floor, out the front and around to the back door?"

"I love the way you think."

THE SHOTGUN WAS FASTENED to a kitchen chair and aimed at the kitchen door. An elaborate system of string and sticks ensured that the minute the kitchen door was half open, whoever was on the other side would get blasted. Half a load from a twelve gauge at a range of four feet is sufficient to cause considerable mutilation, if not death.

"Nice gun," Stryker said in a thin voice. He had been within two feet of opening the door earlier.

Neilson was throwing up into the sink. If he hadn't tripped, he kept gasping between convulsions, if he hadn't gone down onto his face before the thing went off—

"Kind of a dumb setup, seeing the way the door opens," Stryker observed, after a minute. He handed Neilson a towel from the rack. "If it opened out, a person would get the full charge. But it opens in. So why this door? Why only one barrel at a time? Why this whole thing?"

"Somebody doesn't like you," Neilson said, after rinsing his mouth, and washing and wiping his face. "I think it's me."

"It could be," Stryker agreed slowly.

Neilson looked at him over the towel. "I was *joking,* Jack."

"I wasn't," Stryker said. He went over to the hall closet and began to look around for the fire extinguisher he'd bought years ago for just such exciting occasions.

NINETEEN

"ARE YOU *CRAZY?*" Neilson demanded, when the television set had been successfully extinguished. "Of *course* we have to report this, Jack. Somebody set you up, tried to kill you—"

"I noticed," Stryker said drily. He was back on the couch, nursing his aching shoulder with a beer. Internal anaesthesia, an old Indian trick.

"Forensic has to go over the gun, we need pictures..."

"We *need* nothing," Stryker said. "Suppose we just let it all sit there for twenty-four hours—what harm will it do?"

Neilson stared at him. Slowly he sank down on the coffee table, wiping his face with his sleeve. The blood smeared but was not entirely removed. "It will give the bastard another twenty-four hours on the street, for one thing," he said. "Another twenty-four hours to finish you off and maybe somebody else, too."

"I want him," Stryker said.

"Great, sure, we all want him, Jack. And we'll get him. But this time he's varied his pattern and—"

"No, you miss the point. *I* want him," Stryker reiterated.

"Oh shit," Neilson groaned. "Don't give me that."

"Do me a favour—call the hospital, see if Tos is okay," Stryker said. "That much you can do, can't you?"

Neilson stood up. "Right," he said. "And then I call downtown."

"Just call the hospital first."

"All right, all right. I'm calling the goddamn hospital," Neilson said, with the tone and expression of someone humouring a dangerous child. "Here I go—dialling away." After a muttered conversation, he replaced the receiver. "Tos is fine."

"Sure. *Now* call the hospital and make sure."

"But I just—"

"Called Pinsky—now call the hospital, okay?"

Neilson stared at the back of Stryker's head, visible over the back of the sofa that stood in the middle of the room. "You counted the clicks?" he asked.

"No—I read your lips. WILL YOU CALL THE GODDAMN HOSPITAL?"

"Jesus—you sure get grouchy when people shoot at you," Neilson grumbled. This time he got through, verified that Toscarelli was still unconscious but perfectly sound otherwise, and relayed the information to Stryker. "Satisfied?"

"Yeah—now put the phone down."

"Hell with that—I'm calling this in," Neilson said.

Stryker stood up and turned to face him, holding his revolver at waist level. "Put the phone down, Harvey. I mean it."

Neilson stared at him, then replaced the phone in its cradle with a long, disgusted groan. "Oh, Jeeesus, Jack—cut it out."

"We're going to wait for Ned. Sit down, Harvey." Stryker waved the gun towards the easy chair in the corner. The big soft one that was so comfortable—and so difficult to get out of quickly. "Sit down right there."

"I'd like to wash my face..."

"Sit."

Neilson sat.

About ten minutes later, the doorbell rang. They both went to answer it, Pinsky entered, saw Neilson's bloodied face, Stryker's drawn gun, and growled.

"What the hell is this?"

"This is the psycho ward," Neilson said. "He's off his nut."

Stryker waved them into the sitting room with his gun. Pinsky stopped in the doorway and stared. "What the hell?"

"He's been redecorating," Neilson said. "That's what we're supposed to pretend—that he's been redecorating. What do you think of it, so far?"

"It stinks," Pinsky said, wrinkling his nose. "Literally. Look, Jack—I haven't had my dinner, yet, I'm dead beat and—"

"Sit," Stryker said. When they both just stared at him, he repeated it. "SIT DOWN. GODDAMMIT!"

They sat.

Stryker stood in front of them, gun still drawn. His face was white with weariness and pain, and his eyes sparked in the light from the low lamps. "I think a cop is doing this," he said.

They looked at each other, and then back at him.

"You heard me," Stryker said, his voice rising. "A cop. I think it's a cop. It has to be a cop." He waved the gun at Neilson, who almost didn't flinch. "Who else could find out where any officer was at any given time? And that they were alone? Who would know habits, schedules, movements? Maybe he even put false calls through Despatch to draw them to where he could get them. Who else could have a radio to pick up the calls?''

''Almost anybody with the money to buy one,'' Pinsky said calmly. ''You're not making any sense. Put the gun down, Jack, for crying out loud.''

''No, not until you promise to give me time to get the bastard. I want a twenty-four-hour guard on Tos, I want a driver who will do what I say. I want access to the computer, and I want—''

Pinsky stood up. ''I don't give a shit what you want,'' he said angrily. ''Put down the goddamn gun.''

Stryker began to back up. ''I'll shoot you, Ned.''

''Like hell you will,'' Pinsky said. ''I've known you a long time, Jack. Give me the gun and go to bed. We'll handle all this. If it's a cop, if it's whoever—we'll get him. Leave it to us.'' He waved down Stryker's attempted interruption, and he kept coming. ''Don't you think we're good at what we do? Didn't you teach me all you know? Didn't you?'' As he spoke he reached out a long arm and snatched the gun from Stryker's hand. He checked the safety and it was on— as he knew it would be.

He put the gun in his pocket. Gently, he pushed Stryker backwards until he came up against the sofa. Then he pressed on his good shoulder and made Stryker sit down. ''He's just tired,'' he said to Neilson, as if that explained everything.

''He's nuts,'' Neilson said, annoyed with himself for not facing Stryker down. But goddammit, the son of a bitch was scary when he was mad.

''Now tell me what happened,'' Pinsky said to Neilson. Neilson told him. Throughout, Stryker sat on the couch, head down, saying nothing—a man defeated before he'd begun.

When Neilson had finished, Pinsky went out into the kitchen and looked around, then came back in. "I'm phoning this in," he said, reaching for the phone.

"No, don't—" Stryker said.

"Sorry, Jack—you know it has to be done," Pinsky said firmly. "Some rules I'll bend, but not this time. It's for your own good."

"Dammit, listen to me!" Stryker shouted. He reiterated the things he'd said before. "What's more. I think I know who it is. I think it's Tim Leary."

"That's interesting," Pinsky said. His hand was still on the phone, but the receiver remained in the cradle.

"You didn't think it was interesting before," Neilson reminded him.

"He didn't say it was Leary, before," Pinsky said. "He only said 'a cop.'"

"Why should Leary go around killing police officers?" Neilson demanded.

"Because he hates the department," Stryker said. "He hates all of us. You can see it in his eyes. You were in court, Ned. You were at the Bronkowsky trial. You saw how he looks at the rest of us; you must have seen the hate in his eyes. He wants to bring us down but they won't let him testify, so he's taking another route, he's picking us off, one by one, and he's going to go on doing it until somebody stops him."

"I'm not sure I buy that," Pinsky said slowly. "Isn't he under surveillance by IAD?"

"No," Stryker said. "I phoned up and asked."

"Isn't anybody watching him?" Neilson demanded.

"No," Stryker said.

"Jesus—why not?"

"You tell me."

Pinsky and Neilson exchanged a glance. "Friends?" Pinsky postulated.

"He knows things?" Neilson countered.

"Take your pick," Stryker said.

"And you think he did this?" Pinsky asked, gesturing first towards the kitchen and then the gutted television set.

"Who else could do it, for crying out loud?" Stryker demanded. "I'll bet if we track back we can find some connection between Leary and all the officers who've gone down. But he messed up with Tos and me. Twice with me now. And he's probably going to try again. He's crazy—he must be, but he's too smart to let it show."

"Then you and Tos should have protection," Pinsky said.

"Tos, yes, but I don't—" Stryker began, then stopped. From outside there came the sudden sound of an approaching siren.

Neilson went to the window and looked out. "Looks like somebody on the block believes in the good neighbour policy. We got a black and white out front and two uniforms coming up the path."

"Damn, *damn, DAMN!*" Stryker howled.

Pinsky glanced at Neilson. "And just when things were going so *well,*" he said.

TWENTY

THE HOSPITAL ROOM was dark and quiet, save for the hum and click of the machines monitoring the still comatose Toscarelli. Stryker, looking haggard and furtive, slouched across to the chair beside the bed, and sank into it. He looked at Tos's profile, and sighed.

"The thing is, no matter what Pinsky does, he's not going to get anyone over here before morning, is he? That's assuming he gets permission for anyone at *all,*" Stryker said. "So the way it's going to be is, I'm going to sit here until your mother comes, right? I don't think *anybody* can get past your old lady and your sister, Marina. She may look like an angel, but she's got bony knuckles. If I tell her the score even the nurses may have trouble getting to you."

Tos said nothing.

"And if Pinsky can't talk Klotzman into detailing protection, then I'll be back tomorrow night, again. Any objections?"

Apparently Tos had no objections.

"The way I'm thinking at the moment, it looks like Leary," Stryker went on conversationally. "And what I want is, I want to be loose, you know. You know how I like to be loose to move around, right?"

Tos knew.

Stryker told him about all the thinking he'd done, and the phone calls he'd made, sitting in his office during the long afternoon, putting it together. And, finally, he told him about the shotgun. "So I did a number back at the house. When Klotzman came along after all the local precinct boys, and started doing his paternal act, I collapsed with the strain, right? It was pitiful. Neilson had to carry me upstairs. I was a wreck. And then Pinsky called my doctor, who is a very old friend, and he promised Klotzman he would send me to a nursing home out of town, where I'd be safe. That's where I am now, at the nursing home near Philadelphia, resting easy and behaving myself. Look at my face—see how I'm enjoying myself?"

Tos wouldn't give him away.

"'Now, tomorrow, I'm going after Leary for you. I'm going to tag on his ass until he can't break wind without tarnishing my belt buckle. And I'm going to nail him. Goddammit, I'm going to nail him good."

Satisfied that he'd brought his partner up to date on the situation, Stryker sank down onto the base of his spine and dozed off. It was not the sleep of ordinary folk, but the light, listening sleep of new mothers and old cops. His mind had catalogued the noises of the room—any addition, any click, whisper, groan, or step that was out of place, and his brain would jerk him upright with all bells clanging.

He trusted his brain.

But not much else.

"CAN YOU DRIVE?"

Dana stood beside the bed, wrapped in a towel, having left damp footprints all the way from the bathroom.

"Of course I can drive. Who is this?" she demanded.

"Jack Stryker. I'm downstairs."

"Shouldn't you be in bed?" When he didn't immediately respond, Dana gritted her teeth. "That wasn't an invitation, dammit, it was a simple enquiry about your health."

"I feel fine. Could we talk?"

"I don't know if we have anything to talk about. They told me you were off the case."

"Well—I am and I'm not. Mostly, I'm on an involuntary hunger strike. I ordered breakfast but I can't handle it. Could you come down and cut up my bacon for me, please?"

"I see. This is a humanitarian request."

"You could say that."

"Give me a few minutes."

"I'm in the grillroom, table in the corner on the left."

When she arrived she sat down opposite him, pulled his plate over, and began cutting up his bacon. She gave him a glance and scowled. "You sure you don't want me to get someone to chew this for you? You don't look like you'll have the strength."

"My present appearance belies my lightning reflexes and the body of a true athlete, toned to perfection—"

She shoved the plate back. "Shut up and eat."

He did the best he could, while she ordered coffee, orange juice, and an English muffin. When all was consumed, she sat back and lit a cigarette.

"I didn't know you smoked," Stryker said.

"I don't," she said.

"But—" He looked at her grim expression and gave it up. "I'm glad to hear it," he said. "Smoking is bad for you."

"So they say," Dana smoked her cigarette and regarded him with caution. He looked a little wild this morning. Not having known him for very long, she wasn't certain whether this was a variation of normal, or full-blown dingbat. She knew he'd lost a lot of blood and should have been pale, but his eyes were bright—fever bright?—and his cheeks were flushed. She stifled an impulse to feel his brow and take his pulse—considering the look on his face he might knock her flat on her ass if she tried it. Despite his injury, which was obviously bothering him, he had regained that air of suppressed energy and danger she'd noticed when they'd first met. She had a feeling he was trouble, big trouble for everyone, especially himself. Part of her wanted to blow a whistle, part of her wanted to ring a bell. She drew in smoke and tried not to cough.

"Why do you want to know if I can drive?"

"Because I want you to drive for me."

"You're leaving the department and starting a taxi firm?"

"I want to tail a suspect and I can't drive like this." He indicated his arm, still in the sling. She had seen how gingerly he moved it, how still he tried to remain, and how difficult it was for him.

"I thought you were off the case," she said.

"Actually—" he began, then stopped. He fixed her with a manic eye and gave her a large, charming smile. "Actually, I *am* starting my own taxi firm. It should be a lot of fun. And there's a profit-sharing program. Care to partake?"

"What are the hours?"

The charming smile fell off his face. "The hours are until we get him."

"Him whom?"

"Him one Timothy Leary." He gave her the background, his theory, his goal. "At the moment I can't come up with any other answer that makes sense—not one that includes Tos and me on the list of suspects, anyway. Being in the state I'm in—which is Pennsylvania, as it happens, I'm in a nursing home near Philadelphia—"

"Are you, really? Food any good?"

"As long as someone cuts up my bacon I'm doing all right. To follow Leary I need two things—someone to drive for me on the outside, and on the inside I need someone good on computer to make some kind of connection with the victims and Leary—"

"Even if there isn't one?"

He scowled. "Of course there's a connection. There must be."

"Why?"

"Because I say so." The manic gleam in his eye was brighter.

"Because you want to get Leary?"

He saw suspicion in her eyes, and tried to gear down. "Because I want to get the sniper. If Leary isn't it, then we might as well eliminate him." He sighed heavily, and leaned back. "Either way we'd be doing a job of work for the department, for crying out loud. I have a hunch, let's try it out. What the hell else am I good for at the moment, anyway?" he demanded.

"I don't know, but I do know *I'm* good for a lot of things," Dana pointed out. "Number one thing I'm good for is doing the job I was sent to do."

"Do it, then. But do it with me."

She took a long pull on her cigarette, stubbed it out, and contemplated their empty plates. "Who's your man on computer?"

"Neilson."

She raised an eyebrow. "Isn't that a little ... tricky?"

"Very."

"Couldn't he lose his job?"

"Yeah, he could lose his job. So could Pinsky."

"My God, what's Pinsky doing for you?" She looked at him in horror.

He grinned at her. "Pinsky? He's following Suspect Number 2."

TWENTY-ONE

DANA AGREED TO DRIVE HIM only so she could keep an eye on him. Before they started out, however, she excused herself and went to her room "to change."

And telephoned Neilson.

"What should I do?"

Neilson, caught on the hop halfway between pretending to be at his desk and pretending not to be hanging around a computer terminal downstairs in Records, had mixed feelings about advising her. He would have preferred her to come in and help him on the computer search. It would have left him free to come and go and strengthen the impression that he was working upstairs. As it was he was pulling in an old and tenuous favour owed to him by a Records clerk, and he wasn't certain how much further he could take it.

Dana would have been given computer access without question.

On the other hand, to have driven Stryker himself or for Pinsky to have done so would have been even more risky, as it would have been outright defiance of Klotzman's orders to cut Stryker out of the investigation.

Dana was reporting to no one but herself.

On the third hand (things were getting surreal) somebody needed to keep an eye on Stryker, to make sure he didn't get himself shot again or into some other kind of trouble.

Dana was a beautiful girl.

"What do you want to do?" Neilson asked, drawing circles on his blotter.

"Are you getting anywhere in Records?"

"Sort of. Leary was a detective lieutenant assigned to two of the precincts where we've had uniformed victims. Dates put him in with them for at least some time. No connection yet with Yentall. Or with Hawthorne, for that matter. I'm working on it."

"Could I help you there?"

"Sure. It would be a big help if you were here with me. You might even help some with the computer."

"Ha. How about Pinsky—could I do any good with Pinsky?"

"No—he's married.

"Forget it—I'm sorry I called."

"No—wait. I'm sorry, okay? I don't know where Pinsky is at the moment. According to the schedule he's taking a sick day. When I phoned him, Nell said he was still asleep."

"Jack says he's supposed to be following 'Suspect Number 2.'"

"Who the hell is that?" Neilson was nonplussed.

"I don't know." Dana sounded fretful. "Do you think Jack ought to be running around like this? He seems a little—a little—"

"Nutsy?"

"Wobbly."

"In mind or body?"

"Well . . . both."

That made advising her easier. "Stick with him for a while. Call me if it looks like it's getting to be a problem." He gave her the extension of the Records office he was temporarily invading. "If I'm not here, I'm there, okay? But don't tell anyone."

There was a pause. "I know this extension number," Dana said slowly. "I used this office the other day, when I first arrived. The Records officer on this is named Carole, isn't she? Blonde? Sort of—large?"

"Yeah, Carole Schecter. She only comes up to my tie pin."

"I didn't mean large in that way."

"Yeah, well—I didn't say she could get *close* to my tie pin. Jealous?"

"Relieved. You can bother someone else for a change."

He grinned at the phone. "You don't *sound* relieved."

"Good-bye."

He put the phone down, slowly, and smiled at it. "I'll be damned," he murmured softly. "She's worried about me."

"You can smile at that phone all day, Neilson, it won't fall in love with you," Chase said, going by.

"I know—I never did do any good with phones," Neilson agreed absently.

CHARLIE HEFF HAD BEEN a guard in Courtroom number 3 for over twenty years. "I seen 'em come up, and I seen 'em go down," he was fond of saying to anyone who would listen. In his grey uniform and visored cap, Charlie stood by the door, protecting the judicial process.

Fortunately, he had coffee breaks.

The basement cafeteria of the Justice Building was marble-walled, marble-floored, and as noisy as a boilermaker's convention. Over the clatter of cutlery and the crash of plates were overlaid a good fifty separate conversations, rising up and curling around with the cigarette smoke. To those who were accustomed to it, however, the noise was as good as soundproofing. As long as you leaned close, cupped an ear, and had taken a course in lipreading, you were safe to hand over virtually anything, including the number of your Swiss bank account. Stryker and Charlie were old hands. Dana was struggling to understand what they were saying to one another, but she didn't complain.

"Sure, I know who you mean," Charlie said, across the marshmallows that floated gummily on top of his hot chocolate. "Big ugly guy in a cashmere coat. I know Leary from a long time back, from patrolman on up, coming and going in the courts like the rest of you guys to say his pieces. Bad-tempered bastard—beg your pardon, lady. He's not in there now, though."

"Has he been in there at all, today?" Stryker asked.

"Sure, he was there first thing this morning, but he left before lunch. He ain't come back yet, far's I know. What's he done?"

"I don't know if he's done anything, yet," Stryker said. "I just want to get in touch with him. Has he been in court every day of the Bronkowsky trial? He was there when I testified."

"Most days, yeah. Some days he left early, or didn't show up 'til lunch, but most days he showed up. Sucker for punishment. They gonna call him? I hear he knows a lot."

"Oh, he knows a lot, all right. Can you remember which days he was missing?"

"Hell, no. Take more 'n hot chocolate and a doughnut to make me remember that. No, put your damn wallet away. What it would take is a brain transplant or something—you got a spare brain in your pocket by any chance?''

"I don't understand.''

Heff tapped his temple. "Memory's going. Each damn day seems just like the rest, sort of all blends together. Way I remember is, I remember what I had for lunch, see, but that's not always the same, either. I know I had liverwurst yesterday, and meatloaf sometime this week, maybe, but that's as far as she goes. You don't need to remember more 'n a day or two in this job, open a door, close a door, tell 'em where the johns are, tell 'em what's going on inside the court, stuff like that is all I do. They got a name for it, but I can't remember that, neither. Can remember last year, mind you—want to know anything about last year? Year before? I'm your man. Tell you all you want to know about the Dewey campaign, I was a Dewey man, or when I was on the railroad, but—''

"So Leary was absent from court on an irregular basis? That's the best you can say?''

Heff nodded. "Yeah—on an irregular basis. Sort of like my memory, you might say. Sorry I can't help you more, folks. One of the other guards do you? Harry or Pat?''

"No—we've tried them already, thanks. They've only been on number 3 on an—''

"Irregular basis?'' Heff crowed with delight. "Ain't that just the way, now? I'm there all the time and can only remember half of it, they're around half the time and can't remember any of it.''

"Well, thanks for your help—'' Stryker began.

"You could try that cartoon fella,'' Heff said suddenly.

"Cartoon fellow?'' Dana asked.

"Sure. Him that draws for the papers—sits over in the corner of the court and draws everybody. He might be able to tell you which days your man was here and when. Keeps real careful notes, he does, on account of not being able to take pictures, you know? Now *he's* what you might call there on a *regular* basis. Can't think of his name, though."

They thanked him and left. As they went out of the cafeteria they could hear him chuckling to himself about "an irregular basis." It seemed to afford him vast amusement.

They took the artist to lunch at a quieter place than the cafeteria, and Stryker got the dates and timings he was after. When the artist left to return to court, he started to compare them with the dates and timings of the crimes, jotted down carefully in his notebook.

"He could have done the first one," he said, after a moment. "And he could have done Hawthorne, because that was at night, right?"

"Presumably," Dana agreed. She watched as Stryker, still looking slightly feverish, went on flicking over pages, stopping at the relevant entries. It was awkward for him, using only one hand, but she made no move to help. She was in both a good position and a bad one. Her boss in Washington had given her more or less a free hand in order to ascertain what had happened to Gabe Hawthorne, but she was under no illusions that her brief covered helping an injured rogue detective to buck the system.

On the other hand, she was probably already in trouble, so what did it matter? She had opened her soul to a startled Harvey Neilson after years of repression. Why stop at kicking over one set of traces? Why not kick them all over?

"It's him," Stryker breathed. His face was bright with satisfaction. "It's Leary—he could have done them all. Every one of them. He was out of court every single time an officer went down."

"That doesn't prove anything," Dana said quietly. "You only know where Leary *wasn't* at those times. You don't know where he was, do you?"

"That's the next thing we find out," Stryker said, standing up. "Pay the bill, will you?"

"What?"

He gazed down at her and beamed cherubically. "Well, I haven't got much cash, and I can't use my credit card, can I? I'm in a nursing home near Philadelphia, having my forehead stroked by beautiful nurses."

"May they all have dishpan hands," Dana muttered, reaching for her handbag.

TWENTY-TWO

"I DON'T KNOW HOW you do it," Pinsky said, shivering inside his old lumberjacket and chinos. "How can you stand it?"

"You get used to it," Mike Rivera said. "After the first day, you don't feel hungry. After the second day, you don't feel the dirt. After the third or fourth day, you don't feel your feet. And so it goes on. I think that's how it happens to them, too, plus they got the booze to deaden them out." He looked around. "You spotted him yet?"

Pinsky scanned the street, both sides. "Not yet. So, how did you get on to this?" he asked. They were walking along French Street, heads down, the necks of bottles in brown paper sticking out of their pockets, seeming to ignore the life around them. It was not easy to ignore, what with the smells and the moans and the sadness that hung in the air and hit you in the throat. Pinsky certainly felt *something* in his throat—something it was hard to swallow.

Rivera shrugged. "After the boy was killed, I read a lot of books on psychology. Trying to understand, and like that. Carla, she didn't want to understand, she just wound herself up tight in her misery. She was a hell of a good cop, you know. But always too tough on herself, always pushing for that extra inch, that idea she had of perfection. Me, I go with the flow, right? That's why this kind of assignment is good for me. I bend and weave, become part of the scenery.

Anyway, I wanted to know *why* it had happened that
my kid got it and somebody else's didn't. What had
made the killer that way, because he came from a good
background, that bastard. Money in the family, all
that, whereas me, I come from nothing. Right up from
nothing."

"And look where you are now!" Pinsky said wryly.

Rivera looked around and grinned. "Right. Anyway, I wanted to know what made the difference, him
and me, you know? That really bugged Carla, me
trying to work it out, but I figured a good cop should
know that stuff. Anyway, when we finally split up,
well, I had a lot of time on my hands. To keep from
going crazy myself, I started to do volunteer work here
and there. I got to know this street. One day I thought
about how a semipermanent undercover situation
could be real useful, and I told my captain and he said
'try it,' so I'm trying it. So far, so good."

"But, Jesus..." Pinsky couldn't get the words out.

"Maybe that's got something to do with it," Rivera agreed.

"What has?"

"Jesus Christ," Rivera said. "I got a strong faith,
Ned. It helps a lot, having a strong faith, down here.
Being like this. The hard part—the hardest part—is
having to ignore things. I mean, you and me, we're
trained to *do* something if we see pain or crime or
whatever, right? That's why we became cops in the
first place. Here, I just have to let all kinds of crap slip
by. I've seen some things you wouldn't believe, and I
had to do nothing, say nothing, just stand back and let
them go down. I don't know, maybe that's what will
beat me in the end. You do your time at the academy,
work for years trying to uphold the law like they say,

and then end up wearing rags and standing lookout while some pusher does a deal in an alley. I even committed some crimes myself, what do you think of that? But it's part of the cover, part of the game. I hate it, but I have to do it if this thing is going to work, right?''

''Like the crap at the hotel?''

''You mean Feeney taking a 5 percent rake-off on all the food bills? Sure. Like that.''

Pinsky was shocked. ''Does he?''

''What do you mean, does he?'' Rivera looked at him. ''Isn't that what you wanted me to find out about?''

Pinsky shrugged. ''We thought it was more than that.''

''What—10 percent?''

''No, no—something *other* than that. Five percent of damn all isn't enough to kill someone over, is it?''

''Not for you or me, maybe. But down here they kill each other over a pair of shoes. That's life to them, a pair of shoes. When it's all you've got, well, it's your entire fortune, right? Wouldn't you fight to keep your entire fortune—family, house, car, bank account? Sure you would. Well, a pair of shoes is that to them, sometimes. Or a coat, maybe. Or a bottle of booze. Their whole fortune. So they fight. Sometimes, they kill.''

''You're going native, Mike.''

Rivera chuckled. ''I go back to my own apartment every ten days. I got my whole pay to spend on me. Carla has a good job, she doesn't want alimony now, so I got this really great apartment downtown, fixed it all up myself from scratch. I have a bath, I put on clean clothes, I walk around my clean rooms, I eat in

good clean restaurants, I do office work at the precinct house, stuff like that. Ordinary. Like before.
Then I come back here. It's the first day that's hard.
After that, like I said, it gets easier. And I never stay
longer than ten days. Never." He paused and took a
swallow from his bottle. Wiping his mouth on his
sleeve, he spoke quietly. "We been nearly down the
whole street, Pinsky? You sure he's here?"

"Oh, yeah. I think we should go back to where they
had the fire going."

Rivera shrugged. "Suits me." They turned and
made their way back about a block to a vacant lot,
where some of the local denizens had built a fire in an
old rusty oil drum. Through the holes in the sides
could be seen the smouldering glow of burning garbage, and heat pulsed out, causing the air around the
drum to shimmer and waver. Pinsky and Rivera approached slowly and waited until a space opened up,
then they gently moved in and held out their hands.
Pinsky had rubbed his hands in the dirt of his garden
at home before slouching downtown, but his hands
were practically clean next to Rivera's.

"We share," one of the tramps said, eyeing the
brown paper bag in Pinsky's jacket.

"Oh right," Pinsky said, and handed the bottle to
the man next to him.

"I share first," said the man who had spoken, apparently the leader of the little group. He was tall and
bulky, and looked better fed than the others. His face
was heavily boned, and there were thick ridges of scar
tissue on his eyebrows. He might have been an old
prize-fighter, for he had the sullen look of unreason
that a battered brain might produce. He understood

confrontation, he understood dominance—and there it ended.

The man who had taken the bottle from Pinsky hurriedly passed it to the big man, who took a long, long swallow from it, emptying nearly a third of the contents.

"That's a big share," Pinsky observed.

The big man eyed him, his expression hostile. "So?"

Pinsky shrugged. "Nothin'—I just figured everybody would get some, and then I'd get it back, you know?"

"And if you don't?" the big man asked.

"Then he don't," Rivera said quickly. "Listen, Ham—he's new in town. He doesn't know anything about anything, okay?"

"Maybe he should be learned something, then," Ham said, passing the bottle to the man next to him. The recipient quickly drank what he could before the next man grabbed the bottle from his mouth and put it to his own. Soon they were all jostling to get a swallow, but Ham just stood there glaring at Pinsky.

"Sorry," Pinsky said humbly. "Didn't know it was your fire."

"Oh?"

"I mean, if it's your fire, well then, you get more, right?" Pinsky mumbled on. "Took the trouble to make the fire and all that..."

"Where are you from?" Ham demanded.

"Cleveland—he's from Cleveland, he said," Rivera put in.

"Don't they know much in Cleveland?" Ham asked, enjoying himself now that Pinsky had grovelled a little.

Rivera laughed. "They don't know nothin' in Cleveland, that's why he come here, right, Bugs?"

Ham scowled. "Why they call him Bugs?" he asked suspiciously. "He got bugs?"

"Man, we all got *bugs*," cackled a little man in about fifteen layers of shirts and sweaters from which his legs in badly split drainpipe jeans descended like two blue toothpicks stuck into a ball of rags.

"I got no bugs on me," Ham said loudly, glaring at the little man. "I washed last week at the hostel."

"They call him Bugs because he looks like Bugs Bunny," Rivera improvised. The name Bugs had just come to him, and Pinsky gave him a look designed to prevent any such thing ever happening again.

"I don't look like no goddamn bunny," Pinsky said crossly.

"You got big ears," said a hunched, raincoated figure that had joined the gathering just too late to partake of the last of the whisky in Pinsky's bottle. Everybody looked at Pinsky's ears.

"His ears aren't so big," Ham said.

"I didn't mean like size," the newcomer said. "I meant he's got big ears 'cause he's a cop. Isn't that right, 'Bugs'?" The nickname came out riding on a sneer. Everybody in the circle stiffened. "I said, isn't that right?"

Rivera stepped back from Pinsky, as if he'd just heard his companion was a plague carrier. Which, in a way, he was—as far as Rivera was concerned. "Jesus—you're kidding!" Rivera gasped. "I been talking to him for twenty minutes, he never—"

"What did you say?" Ham demanded. "What did you tell him?"

"Nothin', I told him nothin' about nothin'," Rivera said, in desperate tones.

"What did he ask you about?" Ham persisted.

"Nothin'—he didn't ask me nothin'!" Rivera's voice was shrill.

"Did he ask you where you could get anything?" Ham demanded. "Did he ask you about you-know-what?"

"No, no—nothin' like that!"

"What's you-know-what?" Pinsky asked without thinking. Force of habit opened his mouth, and his life fell out.

"You bastard," Rivera said to Pinsky. He shoved him, hard, towards the open street. "Get out of here, you bastard. Go on—get the hell out of here."

Pinsky started towards the street, but the voice of the raincoated figure followed him. "He busted me once," the man in the raincoat said. "Just for walking down the street, the son of a bitch. Just for walking down the goddamn street."

"I don't know what the hell you're talking about," Pinsky said, over his shoulder. "You got me all wrong. I ain't no goddamn cop. You guys piss me off, I'm gonna get another bottle and *I ain't gonna share no more!*"

All the men who had been standing around the oil drum began to follow him. Nobody seemed to be in a hurry. Everybody seemed to know what was coming. Everybody but Pinsky seemed to be looking forward to it.

"So what are you doing down here, cop?" Ham asked, grabbing his sleeve and forcing him to stop.

"I'm not a cop," Pinsky insisted, trying not to sound desperate. He knew a patrol car passed down

French Street every twenty minutes, but he couldn't remember how long it had been since he'd last seen it go by. "That guy is just sour because he needs a drink." He knew it was hopeless, now. They were all around him. It was going to happen. There was nothing he could do but brace himself.

"We all need a drink," somebody said. "If you're a cop, then you got a gun. We could sell that gun. Maybe you got money, too. You got any money on you, cop?"

"Let's see," said Rivera, moving in, fast, before the other eager hands got there. His hand went straight in under Pinsky's jacket and closed on the badge folder. He pulled it out. "Yeah, he's a cop, look at this!" He waved Pinsky's folder so the gold badge flashed in the thin sunlight.

They were on him in a flash.

Pinsky did the best he could under the circumstances—he had a long reach and big fists—but there were too many of them. The big, burly man seemed to be given priority here, too, getting in the best kicks and the best punches, primarily because of superior size and strength. But the others had specialities, too. Scratches and bites began to bleed into Pinsky's clothes as he swung and connected and tried to drag himself away from the clutching hands and the blows. Out of one rapidly swelling eye he saw Rivera capering around the fire, waving his badge and gun in the air.

Pinsky, in the midst of disaster, didn't blame Rivera. What was happening to him had been inevitable from the moment the raincoated man had said the word "cop." Even if he had proven to be innocent of such an accusation, they would have beaten the hell out of him, just for existing, and being new on the street, and on the off chance that if he had enough to buy one bottle he might have enough to buy two. It was bad enough to get beaten up—but to lose gun and badge would have been worse.

Rivera would make sure nobody else got them—and they would find their way back downtown. But even as he went down under a hail of hate-propelled blows, Pinsky knew that was the only help Rivera could give him. What was it he'd said?

It was ignoring things that was the hardest.

On the ground, now, Pinsky saw the raincoated man who had fingered him moving away from the seething mass of filthy clothes and stinking bodies that pulsed around their victim. He tried to crawl out from under, but they were holding his arms and legs and keeping him open for the blows and kicks that were coming in fast. So fast. Too fast.

Now he couldn't see Rivera, either. Maybe he'd gone for help. Maybe he'd seen where the raincoated figure had gone, and had followed him, leaving Pinsky to his fate. Not death—these men would stop short of killing.

But they wouldn't stop far short.

Suspect Number 2 was getting away.

"Oh, shit!" shouted Pinsky, making one last superhuman effort to throw off the weight of men that pinned him down. But it was no good. Everything was turning red and black and the world seemed to be made of noise and snarling faces and kicking legs and pain. He felt the hummocky dirt of the empty lot under his back, felt the sharp edge of an empty can, a rock. Somebody picked up the rock. Somebody lifted it high and Pinsky could see its rough surface gripped in the dirty talons of a stranger who hated him.

And then Pinsky couldn't see anything at all.

TWENTY-THREE

NEILSON WAS getting excited.

Maybe Stryker had something after all. There *were* connections—some pretty tenuous, but connections—between Leary and almost every single victim brought down so far.

He had served in the same precinct as Randolph. He had taught a detection class at the training college which Santosa had attended. Santosa had gotten the top mark, too.

It took a long time to make the connection with Yentall, but when it finally came together, he grinned and patted himself on the back. Leary and Yentall had been in the same graduation class at Madison Heights High School. They had both been on the football team there, too.

Making the connection with Merrilee Trask had taken even longer. Try as he might, Neilson could not make them touch. And then it came—not a direct connection, but a connection. And not with Merrilee Trask, but with her ex-husband, who had been the khaki officer handling administration in Leary's precinct when Leary had been made up to detective sergeant.

And of course, it had been Stryker and Toscarelli who had uncovered Leary during the Bronkowsky investigation.

But he could not make it work with Hawthorne.

Try as he might, all he could come up with was differences. Despite being the same age, they had gone through police training two years apart, because Leary had done two years of college first. They had both grown up in Grantham but on opposite sides of the city, different neighbourhoods, different schools. They had never served in the same precinct or done any courses or cooperated in any interprecinct assignments during the three months that Hawthorne had worked for the department. They had no family or relatives of any kind in common. They had never even attended court on the same days to give evidence.

Of course, in the private areas of their lives that were not covered by the extensive personnel records, they could have met in a hundred ways. They could have used the same barber. They could have bowled at the same alley or done rounds at the same golf courses. They could have shopped at the same supermarket. They could have even met in a gay bar and fallen in love, for all Neilson knew.

Every possibility he thought up, every way in he could think of, resulted in no known connection, or a question mark. From growing excitement Neilson gradually slid into deep depression.

And then they told him about Pinsky.

He'd been uneasy about Pinsky all day. He'd called his home several times, but had no reply after the initial call when Nell had told him Pinsky was asleep. He knew Nell helped out at a local nursery school, and was waiting for her to come home to call again, but then it became unnecessary. He knew where Pinsky was.

In Mercy Hospital.

"WHAT THE JUMPING HELL were you doing on French Street, for Chrissakes?" Neilson demanded of the battered figure on the bed. "Now look at you. Now you *really* got a sick day. Maybe a sick month. Goddammit, Ned, you shouldn't have gone down there on your own. Why the hell did you go down there, anyway?" Neilson was talking and walking in circles.

"I wasn't on my own. I was with Mike Rivera," Pinsky mumbled with some difficulty.

"A fat lot of good *he* was," Neilson growled.

"Couldn't break his cover," Pinsky said.

"Him and Batman."

"He got my badge and gun away," Pinsky said. "They would have got back to you."

"Oh, and I would have been *thrilled* to get them, too," Neilson said. He was really angry. "I could have waved them at the funeral and told everybody how he'd let you go down but the goddamn fucking hardware was safe, right? Saved the city's money, let my partner get the living shit beat out of him. What a hero!"

"Don't shout, Harve, and watch your language. There's sick people here," Pinsky whispered. "One of them is me."

"In the head. In the *head* you're sick, running around French Street. So Big Hero Rivera, the Man of a Hundred Faces, or maybe just two, goes off with your ID, huh? And what if you hadn't woken up in the ambulance? You'd be a John Doe in the charity ward, we'd be looking for you from here to Tuesday, and Nell going up the wall—"

"I didn't know you cared so much, Harve," Pinsky said.

"Care? Who cares, you dumb cluck? Not me."
Neilson was slowing down to a simmer. He stood
glaring out of the window now instead of at Pinsky,
his hands jammed in his pockets. "Who the hell is
Suspect Number 2, anyway?"

"Brother Feeney," Pinsky said. "Rivera said he was
taking a 5 percent rake-off from the suppliers on the
food bills."

Neilson turned from the window and regarded Pinsky's bandaged head with disbelief. "What the hell
has that got to do with knocking off the city's finest,
one by one?"

"Well, it sounds kind of funny, I know, but it's a
theory of Jack's."

"I should have guessed, they're *always* funny,"
Neilson grumbled.

"The way he worked it out, Jack thought he recognised a couple of the guys working at the hostel, and
he checked them out. Pushers, they are. Jack thinks
that the hostel is being used as a distribution centre
and that guys dressed up like bums filter out through
the city and carry the stuff to the street dealers. Who
the hell looks at a bum, he said."

"And Feeney is supposed to be doing this?"

Pinsky tried to shrug, but the strapping on his broken collarbone prevented much movement. "I don't
know. Jack told me you and Dana had found out that
the hostel is owned, through a lot of dummy companies, by that Abiding Light outfit?"

"Oh, yeah—so we did," Neilson recalled. It seemed
a hundred years ago.

"Well, that's probably why Hawthorne was interested in it. Jack seemed to think it was a pretty good

scam, using bums like that to make a network for drugs."

"But is Feeney supposed to be killing our people or what?" Neilson demanded, coming back to the bed to look Pinsky in the face. It was not a pretty sight, but it was one he was glad to see in a bed instead of on a slab.

"Jack didn't say. He just said that maybe what connected all these killings wasn't a person, but a crime. That maybe everybody who got killed had stumbled on this network thing with the pushers, and had to be eliminated. He said stick with Rivera and watch for anybody on the street with red socks. He said he thought that was the key—red socks."

"And did you see anyone in red socks?" Neilson asked.

"I saw three guys in red socks," Pinsky said. His voice was thinning and his eyes closed in exhaustion. "One of them was the guy who told everybody I was a cop."

"THERE HE IS."

Dana looked into the rearview mirror and saw the big man coming out of the house behind the hedge. He was wearing what looked like a cashmere overcoat, and stood about six two in it. His face had once been handsome, perhaps, but now was bloated and pale and sullen.

A woman stood in the doorway, watching him go down the drive towards the car he'd left parked there. She did not wave, and the man did not turn back to wave to her. Neither was smiling.

"Is that his wife?" Dana asked.

"I have no idea," Stryker said. "This is the most recent address given in the files for him, but I don't know what his domestic arrangements are. I wish to hell I could search that car—the rifle might be in there."

"Jack—what possible motive could Leary have for all this killing?"

"He doesn't need a motive that makes sense," Stryker said. "He's turned rotten and he's got nothing to lose. He's also the kind of smart-ass bastard who thinks he's invulnerable, that nobody would be smart enough to catch him. But I'm going to catch him, if I have to hang on his tail for the rest of my life."

"But you—"

Leary had reached his car now, and was searching in his pockets for his keys. The woman had closed the door. The street was deserted, except for some children playing down at the far end of the block. Playing cops and robbers. Stryker glanced at them and smiled. "Bang," they were saying. "Bang, you're dead."

When the shot came, there was a wild instant when he thought it had come from the children, but then Dana screamed.

"Oh God!"

He turned back just in time to see Leary start to slide down the side of his car, half his head blown into a dark spray over the car roof. As he went down, he made a wide, ugly smear on the beautiful white paint of the Mercedes. He hit the ground and sprawled. The smear began to drip down onto him.

Dana was choking and gagging, her hands over her face.

The door of the house opened and the woman who had not waved at Leary stood there, staring out. The hedge obscured her view of Leary's body, but she had heard the shot and Dana's scream, and saw through the leaves of the hedge that the Mercedes hadn't moved.

She looked worried.

Stryker was rigid with disbelief.

Then he heard a noise behind him. A car starting up. He pivoted in the seat and saw a dark sedan pulling out from between cars parked about forty yards behind them. Driving it was a figure in a cap.

"Jesus—there he is!" Stryker shouted. "Start the car, start the car, start the goddamn car!"

As the sedan pulled past the driver glanced briefly in their direction, then gunned the engine and took off down the street. Dana was still rocking back and forth in the driver's seat, her hands over her face.

"STOP THAT! THAT'S HIM—HE'S GETTING AWAY!" Stryker screamed at her, slapping her around the face with his good hand until she stopped sobbing and took in what he was saying. "LET'S GO, LET'S GO!" he screamed.

Too stunned to do anything but what she was told, Dana started the car. As they pulled away, the woman in the door had crossed the lawn to the point where she could see Leary's body.

Her screams blended with the scream of their tyres.

TWENTY-FOUR

"BUT I DON'T KNOW what to *do!*" Dana wailed, as she turned into the road behind the dark sedan.

"Do what I tell you. Don't think, don't hesitate, just do what the hell I tell you to do. You can think about it later," Stryker said, leaning forwards in his seat to try and read the license number. But he could see that the plate was smeared with mud. Nothing missed, the bastard.

But Leary was dead.

It didn't make sense. It didn't make—

"Get ready to turn right, he's going to turn at the next intersection."

"How do you know?"

"He's moving over—there. Step on it, for Christ's sake!"

"The car will turn over if I go any faster!" Dana screamed.

"No, it won't. Don't even think about what the car will do, dammit, don't think at all. Just drive. He's pulling around that car—go for it. *Go for it!*"

She went for it, and narrowly missed a large truck coming at them as she pulled in ahead of the slower-moving compact that had blocked them. "I can't, I can't!" she kept saying, but she went on, her hands gripping the wheel so tightly she thought her knuckles would burst right out through her skin. She felt as if she were standing still and the world was coming at her, faster and faster, some kind of arcade game that had gone out of control. She was terrified, and yet Stryker's voice held her there, locked to the wheel. If she didn't do what he said, if she let go for even one second, the world would explode. She knew it would.

Stryker's voice went on and on, giving her instructions, never giving her a moment to think, to breathe, to be herself. She was an extension of him, of his will; she was a machine and he was running it. "Okay, we're coming up to a big intersection now, and I have a feeling the guy is going to go right through. He could turn left into town, or right out of town, but I think he'll go through towards the freeway. He knows we're after him—dammit, hang a right, hang a right!"

Dana and the tyres screamed together as she jerked the wheel to the right, riding over the corner curbing and causing a woman with a bag of groceries to jump back, scattering tomatoes. One hit the windscreen and made a big red smear in front of Stryker. It made him feel sick for an instant, and then he leaned forward and switched on the windshield wipers, activating the wash at the same time.

"Get closer, get closer, I want some details!" he shouted at Dana over the scream of the engine. The little rented car was not accustomed to such treatment. Why hadn't they taken his, he thought frantically, but he knew why. So Leary wouldn't spot it and report he was being followed and give the license and then Klotzman would find out that Stryker wasn't at the nursing home in Philadelphia, after all. But in *his* car there was a radio. In *his* car he could have called in, gotten help, headed the dark sedan off, boxed him and turned him and funnelled him into a corner.

In *his* car they could have got him.

But they were stuck with this one.

The only thing the radio in this one did was play music.

"Where the hell is he going?" Stryker shouted, frustrated. His mind was spinning with the shock of seeing Leary go down, when all the time he had been convinced that it was Leary who was the sniper. He couldn't get his head clear, he couldn't make sense of it, and there was no time for it now. What was here, and now, like a gift, like a revelation, like God's finger poking him in the eye, was the sniper, dead ahead. And pulling away.

"Faster, dammit—put your foot down!"

"It's down, it's down, it's down!" Dana screamed back at him. "I'm doing the best I can, I can't even feel the car or the road—it's like sliding on ice..." Dana had never driven a car like this, never even approached this speed on city streets. The car felt strange, light, uncontrollable—and yet the least touch on the steering wheel brought a sharp, terrifying response. One touch and they could be off the road into a parked car, or a storefront, or somebody's front yard.

The route the dark sedan had chosen to take was not a busy one at this hour, but there was enough traffic to make their progress erratic and extremely dangerous.

"He's got to be a cop," Stryker muttered, still clinging to his theory as if it were a strap to keep him upright. "Who else but a cop could drive like that?"

The dark sedan had cut through the narrow gap to put three cars between them. One of them was a van, and obscured their view almost entirely. "Pass them, pass them!" Stryker shouted.

Dana was too terrified to take her eyes off the road, but she didn't think he could see what she saw. "How can I pass, there's traffic—"

"Go on the inside—look—there's no parked cars along here, it's ... go on the inside, dammit! DO IT NOW!"

She did it. With a blare of horns—one of them their own—she swerved inside the line of traffic and shot past the two cars and the van. The other drivers, startled, swerved away and then swung back. As she pulled into line ahead of them she hit the leading car a glancing blow. "Keep going, keep going!" Stryker screamed in her ear.

"This isn't a police car!" Dana screamed back, tears covering her face, spreading in the rush of wind from the open window. "I can't keep this up—I can't, I can't!"

"You have to! There, go in there ... Shit! He's turning, he's turning, he's ..."

She saw the dark sedan cutting across a corner gas station, and without hesitation, she went for it. So hysterical was she, so keyed up by Stryker's screams and orders that she just did it.

And missed.

Their front fender caught a stand of oilcans displayed by the pumps, and sent it flying towards the plate-glass window of the station. The impact, small as it was, was sufficient to deflect their course, and she sideswiped a car placed for sale with a cardboard sign in the windshield showing the price.

There was a loud report as their front tyre suddenly blew under the stress of the turn, and the steering wheel was whipped out of Dana's hand as they spun and then slewed sideways across the remainder of the forecourt and slammed broadside into the white fence that separated the station from the line of houses beyond.

Dana was thrown against the door, and Stryker was thrown against her, their bodies straining against their seatbelts. Stryker's head narrowly missed the steering wheel, and had the window not been open beside her, Dana would have smashed into it. As it was, neither lost consciousness for more than a second or two.

In the terrible silence that followed the noise of the crash, Stryker reached out and turned off the ignition. Through the crazed windscreen he could see the dark sedan, disappearing around a curve in the highway.

And then it was gone.

TWENTY-FIVE

"I'M SORRY, I'm sorry, I'm sorry," Dana said sobbing.

"Forget it," Stryker said gruffly. "You did pretty well at that—the guy was ready for us, that's all. Probably had the route planned and everything, just in case."

"But—"

"No, forget it," Stryker said, staring out of the taxi window as they drove towards the hospital. He had used his badge far too much at the gas station, talked big about pursuing a thief, impressed the attendant enough not to call the local precinct cops, and had done the rest by phone. Of course the local cops would be there by now, drawn by the noise and the traffic jam and complaints of drivers they had upset during their chase. They would be going crazy trying to sort it all out. It was only a matter of time before his name and badge number got through to Klotzman. Maybe Klotzman would figure it was just an accident. Maybe. But he'd face that problem when it came up and slapped him in the kisser.

Right now, what concerned him was square one.

And why the hell they were back on it.

The taxi pulled up in front of the hospital. Dana got out, wiping her face with her hands like a child. Stryker paid off the cabbie and they went in.

They sat in the Emergency Room for some time, watching people come and go, before Stryker spotted the intern who had treated him for the gunshot wound. He stood up and waved. The intern stopped short at the sight of him. "Somebody put another hole in you?" he asked.

"No, but I might have opened up the old one," Stryker said. "It feels sticky under there. And this lady isn't feeling so good, either. I think she needs a tranquilizer."

The intern looked at Dana. "You shouldn't hang around with cops, lady. Look what happens to you."

"It was a car accident," Dana said. "I was driving."

The intern raised an eyebrow and looked from one to the other and back again. "And I thought *my* life was exciting," he said. "Come on—we have a special two-for-one sale on today."

"Hey! What about me, I been waiting an hour here," shouted a man with one leg stuck out in front of him encased in a dirty walking cast. "Somebody is supposed to take this off me."

The intern glanced over at him and then pointed to a glass-covered case that housed a fire axe. "If you're in a hurry you can do it yourself," he said. "Otherwise bleeding takes priority over unveiling."

"Crummy hospital!" the man shouted, as they disappeared through the cheerful flowered curtains. "I'll sue!"

The intern's voice floated back from the cubicle. "Forms for lawsuits are at the desk—we run off a fresh batch every morning."

THROUGH BULLYING COMBINED with logic, Neilson had gotten Pinsky moved into the same room as Toscarelli. "Look," he'd said to the nurses and the doctors and finally the managers. "They're friends, they're buddies. Ned can keep talking to Tos. You said people should keep talking to him, right? Well, his mom and his sister go home at night, right? So suppose Tos wakes up in the night and nobody notices? You can't spare nurses to sit around on the off chance, can you? Of course not. But if Ned were there, talking away—" He'd gone on and on in this vein until, fed up with the sound and sight of him, they'd done as he asked.

Since Pinsky had been unable to get police protection for Tos, this seemed to keep two birds alive with one stone. Not that Ned could do much if somebody tried to bump Tos off.

"But you could yell," Neilson pointed out.

"Not until tomorrow," Pinsky rasped through his bruised lips. "No yelling until tomorrow."

"Whatever," Neilson said. He'd had supper in the hospital cafeteria and was wondering if they could put in a third bed for him. His stomach felt distinctly like it needed immediate and sympathetic treatment. He belched.

"Oh, very nice," Pinsky muttered. "What a classy visitor I've got here."

"You want me to go?" Neilson asked irritably.

"No," Pinsky admitted. Toscarelli's mother and sister and his own wife, Nell had departed for home. "Turn on the lights, will you? I hate it when it gets gloomy."

Neilson stood up and turned on the lights. In his bed, Tos grimaced and then his face smoothed out again into blankness.

"Hey—did you see that?" Neilson said in delight.

"He did it before," Pinsky said. "While you were having dinner, they came in to take his pulse and that, and he did the same thing. The nurse said it was a good sign."

"Hot damn," Neilson said, as pleased as if he had done it himself. "Maybe the son of a bitch is in there after all." He leaned over the bed. "Hey, you guinea bastard, wake up, will you? We got work to do, we got to roll, baby, we got to roll!"

But there was no response.

Neilson went on for a few minutes, but finally gave up in defeat. He returned to Pinsky's bedside and dropped into the chair. Pinsky eyed him as well as he could through the swelling. "You got to keep on at it," Pinsky said. "I talked to the nurse and she said we should make some tapes or something, stuff he likes, talking, music, all kinds of things. It's always a familiar sound that gets through to them. Something they're used to hearing. Maybe we should do a tape of the Squad Room or his favourite restaurant." The prospect seemed to exhaust him. "I'm gonna talk to him a lot tomorrow. When it doesn't hurt so much to breathe."

"Good. You do that," Neilson agreed wearily. He had practically dozed off when Stryker and Dana appeared, looking rather the worse for wear.

"What the hell?" Stryker said, stopping stock still in the doorway. He had expected only to see Toscarelli. The sight of Pinsky there, too, battered and bandaged, with Neilson slumped in a chair beside him, was a shock. Neilson, jerked awake by the sound of his voice, peered over the white mound of Pinsky's stomach.

"Hi," he said. Then, seeing Dana, he stood up. "Hi," he said. "What's wrong?"

Stryker told them what was wrong.

Neilson got a chair for Dana and settled her in it. He stood beside her with his hand on her shoulder as Stryker concluded his tale. His face grew more and more stormy as Stryker gave the details of their chase. "She's not trained to do that kind of stuff!" he said, outraged. "You didn't have any right to make her do that."

"I didn't have any choice," Stryker said.

"And I wasn't good enough," Dana said in an exhausted voice. "It should have been you, Harvey. Or Ned."

"You did fine," Stryker said, for the umpteenth time. "I told you, you did all anybody could do." He walked over to the bed and gazed down at Pinsky. "What happened, Ned?"

"Aw, I got beat up a little," Pinsky said dismissively.

"Three broken ribs, a broken collarbone, a broken arm, a bruised spleen, concussion, and numerous contusions," Neilson listed, through clenched teeth. "All because of red socks."

"Sorry, Ned," Stryker said. "I seem to be striking out everywhere."

"No, no—I think you were maybe right about the red socks. I mean, the odds against three bums wearing clean red socks on any given block in the city must be pretty high, and I definitely saw three guys wearing red socks coming from the hostel. I think maybe you're on to something there, Jack."

"Well, then we'd better turn it over to Narcotics," Stryker said.

"So much for all my computer time," Neilson moaned. "Just when it looked like we had something, our prime suspect gets blown away with the rest of the pack. I'm telling you, it isn't fair."

"You got connections?" Stryker asked, going over to look into Toscarelli's face.

"I got a hatful," Neilson said, and listed them.

Stryker was silent, looking at Toscarelli. "That's good, Harvey. That's great. The trouble is, I was wrong—it wasn't Leary, after all."

"Au contraire, mon cher lieutenant," Neilson said. "The lab turned up Leary's prints on the shotgun that killed your television set. *That* was his little setup, all right. I figure maybe he thought it would be put down to the cop killer and left at that. Your backdoor lock isn't exactly up to regulation, you know. No trouble getting in for an experienced bastard like Leary."

"But he wasn't the sniper," Stryker said glumly.

"Nevertheless, there are connections between Leary and all the rest of the victims," Neilson insisted.

Stryker shook his head. "So what? I'm beginning to think that if you start looking at people as hard as we've been looking at them, you could eventually make connections of some kind between every single human being in the world. After all, they all became cops, didn't they? They were bound to be alike in some ways, to have things in common in some parts of their lives. But if there's a winning combination, we sure as hell haven't found it yet." He sighed heavily, looking down at his partner. "Who was it, Tos? Hey? Come out of there and tell us the answer. We got seven cops somebody wanted dead. Five of them are down, you're in there somewhere, and the other one is climbing the wall. Who did it?"

"You've got a big choice," Pinsky said. "Maybe it's something they all did. Or maybe it's like Rivera said—maybe it's something they all *didn't* do."

"What's that supposed to mean?" Neilson demanded.

"Rivera said what?" Stryker asked, turning away from Toscarelli and staring at Pinsky.

"He said the hardest part of working undercover is ignoring the stuff that goes down right in front of you," Pinsky said patiently. "Looking the other way, pretending it doesn't matter. *Not* being a cop. Like that."

"Bad cops."

It was a whisper—not very loud, not very steady, but audible.

The voice was Toscarelli's.

TWENTY-SIX

"BUT, GODDAMMIT, I'm *not* a bad cop," Stryker said adamantly.

"Somebody thinks so," Neilson observed. "Everybody's entitled to their opinion, right?"

They had settled down after the brief flurry of excitement over Tos's first words. Having communicated them to the nurse, celebrated them, and tried for more (unsuccessfully), Stryker had now begun to resent them.

"Well, you've tried everything else," Pinsky said, sounding a bit pissed off. It was late. They kept *talking* and they wouldn't go away. "Why not?"

"I can see Leary qualifying, that's for certain," Stryker agreed. He glanced at the clock, wondering how close Klotzman was to connecting his accident with the reports of wild driving near the scene of a murder. Their path, if traced back, would lead straight to the scene of Leary's death—and some nasty questions. "But what about the rest?"

"Yentall was sloppy," Neilson said. "That came over loud and clear. Trask was a bully."

"Randolph was one of those dreamy types, always looking for a way to coddle the criminal," Pinsky put in while trying to find a cool, comfortable place on his pillow.

"And Santosa was afraid," Dana said morosely. Even when Tos had seemed to surface for a moment, she had remained in her chair, quiet, downcast. She felt very much like Santosa at that moment. She was ashamed of her performance during the unsuccessful chase, bitterly disappointed at having lost the killer and let Stryker down. She knew she wasn't trained in pursuit driving. She was a federal investigator not a proper policewoman, but she felt, somehow, that she should have been able to handle it.

"I don't think that's being a bad cop," Harvey said, perceiving instantly her self-comparison with Santosa. "Not *bad*, exactly. Just inexperienced. We're all afraid when we're on the street—it's one of the things that keeps us alive. And you can't get streetwise overnight, you know. It takes time. He would have been all right." You'll be all right, he was saying, and they both knew it. Dana smiled at him, a little, then looked down at the floor again.

"Okay, fine, they all had faults," Stryker agreed. He went over to stand beside Tos again. "So tell us the rest of it, smart ass," he said with affectionate belligerence. "Open your eyes and tell me all about it, why don't you?"

Tos opened his eyes. He smiled at Stryker.

But he didn't say anything.

After a while, his eyes closed again.

Stryker wanted to burst into tears. He wanted to forget all about the killer and the world and just sit there and wait for Tos to come back home. "I'm not a bad cop!" he said, rather loudly, to the sleeping man. "You're not a bad cop, either! You're just a damn dopey one, lying there like a big cannelloni. Come on, give us the answers."

But there came none.

"I still think it's what Rivera said," Pinsky observed, after some contemplation of the ceiling. He was getting very tired and he wished fervently that they would all go and continue their conversation somewhere else. After all, he was the patient here. He and Tos should get some sleep, shouldn't they? He was a sick man, he was broken and bruised, and he deserved some consideration.

They all looked very small and far away, like puppets on a stage—Dana sitting in the chair, Neilson standing beside her. Stryker bouncing around on the balls of his feet, looking for inspiration anywhere he could find it.

Pinsky found it on the ceiling.

"I think you should find something they all did wrong—intentionally or unintentionally—and see where it takes you," he said in a faraway voice. "Like, say, breaches of discipline, for instance. Maybe they all mouthed off about the same thing or the same person at the wrong time or place. Or maybe you could stop looking at people they put away, and look instead at the ones they didn't. Or maybe they all got mixed up in politics." He was beginning to feel lightheaded from all the painkillers and the talking. "Or periods of absence—how about like they were all picked up by flying saucers at the same time and sent back to spy on earth and now that the aliens have no more use for them, they're bumping them off. How about that?"

"Rivera didn't say anything about flying saucers, Ned," Stryker said. "Get some sleep."

"I *told* you," Pinsky said, with his eyes closed. "I *told* you what he said. Rivera said the hardest part of working undercover is—"

"The things you *don't* do," Stryker finished. He looked at Pinsky and spoke sharply. "What colour were Rivera's socks?"

Pinsky opened his eyes and looked at him, momentarily startled. "Rivera's socks?"

"Yeah."

Pinsky thought back to lying on the ground with everyone on top of him. Looking through the forest of legs and seeing Rivera's filthy trainers prancing around the fire as he waved the gold badge and gun so he, Pinsky, could see they were safe. "White," he said, and closed his eyes again. "Filthy dirty white." He sighed. "I'm going to sleep now."

"Come on," Stryker said. Something in his tone made Neilson suddenly straighten up. "Come on, we've got to sneak into Records. See you tomorrow, Ned."

"Why sneak in?" Neilson wanted to know as they went out the door into the long, silent hospital corridor. Stryker's answer echoed back into the room.

"Because Klotzman may be looking to arrest me."

Pinsky smiled, his eyes still closed. "Good-bye," he whispered. "Goodnight. Sleep tight. Don't let the bedbugs bite."

There was silence.

Pinsky had found peace at last.

It was their problem now. He was out of it. He was off the case. He had no more responsibility, no more problems. He could sleep all night. All night.

"I want a drink of water," announced Tos.

TWENTY-SEVEN

THEY HAD MADE IT into Records without too many people seeing them. And those they saw paid them no attention. There had been a small uprising of dissident students protesting something or other on the university campus down the block, and there was a constant going and coming of cops, reporters, captive students, concerned parents, and university personnel who had seen it all before and would see it all again.

The resulting chaos in the lobby of the Hall of Justice had allowed them to filter through the crowd quite easily.

Neilson's friend was off duty, it being past midnight by now, but they found an empty cubicle and a deserted VDU.

"I still think you're crazy," Neilson whispered as they crowded around the screen. He was cracking his knuckles like a concert pianist about to commence a masterwork. "What are we looking for again?"

"Eberhardt," Dana said. "Somebody named Eberhardt."

"But you can't be serious about Rivera," Neilson protested. "I mean, he's like a legend in his own time, Jack. He's won all kinds of citations. He's a cop's cop. Doing all that undercover—"

"Yeah," Stryker agreed. "Doing all that special undercover which means nobody knows where he is or what he's doing at any given time. He's also got a reputation as a marksman, right? Won a lot of inter-departmental trophies?''

"So I've heard," Neilson conceded.

"And a psycho named Eberhardt killed his son. Do you remember Eberhardt?"

"Not very well—I was out in Madison Heights at the time you and Tos finally put him away." Neilson got out his cigarettes. He offered one to Dana, who shook her head, her eyes on the VDU screen. Neilson saw the smudges under her eyes and the paleness of her skin, and knew she was practically out on her feet. He also knew she wouldn't sit down until she fell down—not after what she saw as her failure in chasing the killer's car. You're going to snap, lady, he said silently. You aren't as tough as you want to think you are, and you're going to go down if you aren't careful. But I'll be there, don't worry. I'll be there.

As Neilson's fingers danced over the keys, Stryker went on, his voice dull with exhaustion. "We put him away, all right, but not for long enough," Stryker said, as Neilson started pulling up records. "We only got him convicted on a count of assault/rape."

"But what about the murder of Rivera's kid?"

"We couldn't *prove* it. It was as clear as the nose on your face, but we couldn't get enough proof. The girl he tortured and raped managed to get away before he killed her. The method he used to torture her was the same method that killed the Rivera boy. But there was no goddamn proof it was Eberhardt. We tried hard, the labs tried hard, but in the end there wasn't enough and the DA went for the lesser charge just to get Eberhardt off the street. Eberhardt was as scum as they come—torture was his line. But he was too smart to get caught—at least, that's what he maintained—too smart and too lucky. He'd been to good schools, he was a rich man's son, he was special—to himself. He bragged about all the times he'd slipped out of our clutches. I want to find out about those times. Here it comes now.''

They watched in silence as Eberhardt's record came up on the screen.

"Oh my God," Neilson breathed. "They're all there."

And they were.

Yentall and Hawthorne were the first—they'd arrested Eberhardt for a juvenile offense, but the arrest had been thrown out on a technicality—Hawthorne had failed to Mirandise and Yentall had let it happen.

Tim Leary had arrested him on a charge of assault, then changed his testimony, claiming that on reflection he was not sure of his identification. "Probably bought off," Stryker said.

Merrilee Trask had beaten Eberhardt up after taking him in on a suspicion of wounding with intent, and the defense had used this to declare his "confession" void.

Sandy Randolph had collared him on a drunk and disorderly after a wild party had drawn complaints, then got the judge to refer him for psychiatric assessment. The shrinks had let Eberhardt off after a month. He had a very high IQ according to all their tests. They said he was not psychotic, just "misunderstood."

Richard Santosa had identified Eberhardt as possibly having committed an assault on a minor—but

he'd let him get away after a brief chase. He'd identified him, but there was no corroborating witness. The
child victim had become an emotional cripple because of her terrifying experience, and could not testify.

Stryker and Toscarelli had failed to get proof
enough to jail him for the murder of David Rivera,
and had to settle for a lesser charge just to get him off
the streets.

"I just can't believe it," Neilson said.

"I can," Dana said. "Sins of omission—Washington thrives on them."

"I can believe it, too," Stryker said. "Leary aside,
none of these cops were 'bad' cops—not in the criminal sense of the word. But they were brutal, or lazy, or
softhearted, or frightened—and the result was that one
vicious piece of crap who started out as a juvenile of-
fender began to believe that he could get away with
whatever he felt like doing. Every time he slipped away
from us—for whatever reason—added to his fantasy
and egomania. Finally he killed—and *still* we couldn't
get him."

"What you're saying is that all these cops were human," Neilson said. "They had moments when they
failed. That doesn't mean they failed all the time."

"Of course not," Stryker agreed. "Just at the
wrong times, with the wrong man."

"Where's Eberhardt now?" Dana asked in a dull
voice.

"Let's see. He should still be in—oh, shit." Stryker

stared at the screen, willing the words to go away. But they stayed, bright green and steady.

"They'll be releasing Eberhardt at nine o'clock tomorrow morning," Stryker said.

TWENTY-EIGHT

THE MORNING HAD ARRIVED filled with the soft primrose promise of spring. Nature was being extremely considerate. An hour of rain before dawn had washed the streets clean, and a light breeze had dried the pavements, so that early pedestrians would not get their feet wet. The air smelled wonderfully fresh—you could sense the green of new leaves and grass with every breath.

Neilson and Stryker had spent most of the night patrolling French Street, hoping for a glimpse of Rivera, but had been unsuccessful. Now they sat, baggy-eyed and gritty, in the front seat of Neilson's car, watching the gates of the prison.

Dana, who had slept on the backseat for most of the night, was fresher of eye if not of clothing.

"What does he look like?"

"Eberhardt or Rivera?"

"Eberhardt."

"Small, skinny, blond, with acne. Long-fingered hands, sort of a sloping walk, like a sneaky rabbit."

"Sounds lovely."

"Rivera, on the other hand, could look like anything at all," Stryker went on. "As Harvey said, he's a master of disguise. He's about five ten, olive-skinned and dark-haired, but that doesn't mean much. He could be anybody walking by here, right now. That's the problem."

The church clock behind them suddenly rang the hour. As the bell tolled out the count, the small door in the larger prison gate opened, and a few diffident men began to filter out. Their steps were uncertain and slow, and they seemed to hesitate for a moment before finally committing themselves to the open space in front of the gates. The third one out was Eberhardt, grinning broadly.

"Over there!" they all said simultaneously. The difference was, Stryker and Neilson meant Eberhardt.

Dana meant the killer.

They all got out of the car at once, heading towards their different objectives, not noticing that they were dividing their forces, because each thought the others were with him or her.

It was a lovely morning. They were tired and they thought the end of their quest was near. Only a matter of minutes, and it would all come right.

It happens.

As Stryker and Neilson walked towards the small group of men who had emerged from the prison, a shot rang out. Twenty yards ahead of them, Eberhardt, no longer smiling, was thrown back against the prison gates by the force of the bullet, which entered his head just above the eyebrows, and exited through the back of his skull to hit the brick of the gateposts, causing a shower of brick dust and chips to mix with the blood.

"Damn!" Stryker shouted, and whirled to see where the shot had come from.

"No!" shouted Neilson at the same time, for he had seen Dana going through the gates of the large cemetery that extended to the left of the church across the way. She was running.

Dana had spotted the figure in the graveyard, perched on top of a small mausoleum behind an almost life-sized figure of the archangel Michael. She saw the rifle, and she saw it jerk as it was fired once. The spring sun glinted for a moment off the telescopic sight as the dark figure stood up and then jumped down, leaving the rifle behind, its work apparently completed.

Dana ran across the graveyard, her shoes squelching in the spring-luscious mud between the graves. The fresh young grass was slippery, for the graveyard walls had prevented the breeze entering the place of mourning. Breezes weren't welcomed there, nor were any other intruders encouraged.

But one had come in.

And now two were running through.

Dana kept her feet, and the grass—for all its surface treachery—muffled her steps, so that she was nearly upon the fleeing figure in jeans, brown jacket, and cap, before her approach was audible.

The killer whirled and saw her.

Suddenly, from beyond the graveyard walls there came the rise and fall of the prison siren.

"Oh, Christ," panted Neilson, stumbling over a gravestone and nearly going down. They had left the fallen Eberhardt surrounded by the stunned figures of his recent fellow prisoners and the guards who had poured out of the prison.

"Which way did he go?" Stryker gasped, aware even as he spoke of the old-time western connotation of his statement. Was there nothing left anyone could say that didn't mean something else? If Neilson said "Thataway" he'd put him on report.

"Over there," Neilson said. "Beyond that black thing."

The black thing was an expensive Victorian-style marble mausoleum, endowed by a family long since without progeny, and therefore sealed. On the other side of it was a small grove of trees and bushes, untended and wild, purposely left untended to serve as a screen to separate the graveyard from the industrial site beyond. In between the graveyard and the soup factory there ran a small stream that flowed into the Grantham River further downtown. It was the same tributary, in fact, that ran behind the hostel on French Street, five miles away.

For most of the year it was merely a muddy trickle, but now, in the spring, it was deeper, faster, and slightly cleaner. In fact, the rain before dawn had already begun to raise its level as it drained from the surrounding hills.

Dana saw the running figure ahead of her dodge between the trees and slip through a gap in the broken fence that edged the stream. Her own clothing was already torn in a dozen places, and she had fallen twice. Blood ran down from one knee, and her hair was in her eyes, but she kept going.

She would not be afraid, like Santosa.

She would not let herself be afraid, ever again.

She, too, slipped through the gap, and found herself on a sloping bank of almost perfectly smooth mud that ran down to a silvery snake of water below. The only marks in the mud were those of running feet. And she knew who they belonged to. Kicking off her treacherous shoes, she started to slither after, being careful to take note of the path of the stream, the possible directions which her quarry might take, the depth of the water, and other details, for her report later.

She would not be sloppy, like Yentall, or secretive, like Hawthorne.

Ahead of her, staggering through the fast-running water, was the brown figure, now muddy and dishevelled. Glancing back, Rivera's mad eyes widened as they perceived Dana, still there, still coming.

Dana entered the water, which came to mid-thigh, and began to run as best she could, the water dragging at her, willing her to go down into its icy rush. Fortunately the bottom of the stream had been scoured of its winter garbage by the increased flood from previous spring rains, but there were still obstacles hidden beneath the surface. One of them caught at Rivera, who went down in a splash and flurry of water. Dana gained ten feet before the killer was up again. Dana kept on.

She would not be forgiving, like Randolph.

Behind her, had she glanced back, she would have seen Stryker and Neilson standing by the broken fence, staring after her as she made her dogged way after the fleeing killer.

"She's not armed," Stryker said.

"She's crazy," Neilson said, and was suddenly afraid, terribly afraid that something would happen to Dana. He hadn't known anything could hurt him so deeply, so terribly, as that thought. They started after her, slipping and sliding, their greater weight causing them to sink more deeply into the mud, to founder and stagger, as in a nightmare where every step weighs a thousand tons, and there is not breath enough nor time enough to evade disaster.

Neilson, younger and fitter, soon pulled ahead. Stryker, off balance with his injured arm, and weakened, came on doggedly behind him. At least they both had guns. But to draw them now, to try and run with them at the ready, was to risk losing their balance and having both their guns and themselves rendered useless by the mud.

So they moved on and waited for their chance.

All they had to do was to get close enough—and make sure Dana wasn't in the line of fire.

The running figures ahead of them rounded a curve and were out of sight for a few minutes. When they themselves rounded the same curve, the riverlet stretched ahead of them, seemingly empty, the banks on either side sloping down, with fences above and the roar of traffic beyond them.

There was no sign of either Dana or Rivera.

"What the hell?" Stryker shouted as he caught up with Neilson. The purling gurgle of the water swirled around their legs. "Where are they?"

Neilson, stunned, looked right, left, back, forth, even up—then gave a shout. "There!"

And Stryker saw them.

Two figures, coated from head to foot in grey, gleaming mud, were struggling in the shadow of an old concrete bridge that crossed the river, about twenty yards ahead.

And it was impossible to tell which was which.

Above them passed trucks and cars in the morning rush hour, oblivious of the struggle that was going on beneath their very wheels.

Dana was strong, stronger than she had ever known she could be, as strong as Merrilee Trask.

But she would not be brutal, like Trask.

She had thrown herself headlong at Rivera as they reached the bridge, and they had gone down together. The mud here was softer, slimier, and they had rolled together in its gummy grasp, one struggling for a hold, the other for freedom. Dana grabbed and clutched, losing her grip and regaining it, only to lose it again and again.

She must not let her prey slip away, like Stryker and Tos.

Her hands gripped slimy clothing, only to have it squidge and squirt from her grasp. She cursed and was cursed in turn, and still the struggle went on. They moved ahead, fell back, turned, floundered, turned again.

Beneath her hands Rivera's sinewy muscles were like snakes beneath the cloth, writhing and shifting. Suddenly Dana lost her balance, and went down under the water, thrashing and struggling. Immediately, quick as snakes striking, strong hands held her down, but she, too, was coated with the mud and slipped free, bursting up from beneath the water with a shout and grabbing what she could.

It was a leg.

Now Rivera was down, but beside the moving water, not in it, twisting and squirming in the mud which made terrible, hungry sucking noises as it tried to swallow them. It stank with an ancient stench of dead

things and sewage and time, and in places it was so
soft, so willing to take them in, that it was almost like
quicksand, eager to accommodate itself to their every
movement. Year in, year out, this small stream had
flowed quietly, untouched, unnoticed, silently ac-
cepting the bits of detritus thrown into it and swept
down to it. It was a lonely stretch of water, without a
name that anyone could remember. But it was not
alone now.

Now it had prey.

Now it could feed.

Dana could feel herself sinking down into the thick,
heavy mud, and was suddenly afraid that it would
close over her, over them both, and no one would ever
know they were down there, in the dark, caught alive
in the wet and the dark.

"No!" she screamed, and wrenched herself away
from its slimy grasp, dragging Rivera with her, away
from the terrible gleaming trap of the silvery grey mud
of the bank and into the firmer, cleaner centre of the
stream.

Rivera, apparently more afraid of her than of the
mud, tried to regain the bank, but Dana held on. It
was like trying to contain the mud itself, for they were
totally coated now. It was in their hair, in their ears, in
their noses and mouths, it had penetrated their clothing and flowed around their bodies like grey grease.
Because of its treacherous lubrication, any hold was
momentary, and every moment of triumph a fleeting
one.

Stryker and Neilson, coming towards them, heard
the gasps and grunts and screams of rage. They drew
their guns but were afraid to fire. They shouted as they

drew closer, but the struggle was primal and desperate, and they were unheard.

Stryker drew his gun, ready to fire.

Neilson, slightly ahead of him, tried to run but the water dragged at his legs and thighs and held him back. As he drew closer he reached out to grab the pair and try to break them apart.

But, with one final and encompassing swirl of mud and water, Dana at last got her arms fast around her captive. She didn't know, then, she was never to know, whether she had truly won or whether her opponent had simply given in, weak, weary, sick of trying. She only knew it was over.

She saw Stryker and Neilson then, and grinned at them, her teeth white and feral in the black mask of mud. "Mirandise!" she commanded.

Stryker, shivering in the wet, began, "Michael Rivera, I warn you that—"

"No!" Dana shouted. "No! Do it right!"

There would be no more mistakes.

Bending down, she forced the face of her prisoner into the water and rubbed it, then pulled off the tightly fitting cap. Long streamers of dark, shiny hair tumbled out. The face washed clean by the water was blank, mad-eyed, and female.

"Jesus Christ!" Stryker said, and could not speak again.

It was Neilson who finally did it.

"Carla Rivera, I must warn you that—"

TWENTY-NINE

DANA STOOD, a slight and mud-caked figure, as they took Carla Rivera away. She went peaceably enough—her self-imposed "mission" was finished, after all.

"I told you that policemen's wives can hate the department worst of all," Dana told Stryker.

"But she *was* a cop," Neilson protested. He'd just come back from putting out an APB for Mike Rivera. Divorced or not, he thought Rivera would probably want to look after his wife.

"I know. Which made her a very dangerous proposition," Dana said. "She was trained to kill, and knew all the ways to avoid getting caught. We have always had a problem with returning soldiers, for the same reason. Thank God most of them know the difference—whatever the difference is."

"Why couldn't she just have shot Eberhardt and be done with it?" Neilson grumbled. "She would have been doing us all a favour. He was a repellent little bastard—God knows what he would have done if he'd been left to run the streets. Instead she takes out decent cops."

"Shooting Eberhardt was just as wrong as shooting our men," Stryker said. "Our job is catching criminals—not making judgements, Harvey. She was as wrong to judge Eberhardt as she was to judge the officers she killed."

"Just bag 'em and tag 'em, hey, Lieutenant?" Neilson said sarcastically. "And the rest is up to the courts? Jesus—don't you get sick of that same old song?"

"No, I don't," Stryker said evenly. He knew it sounded pious. He also knew it to be, for all sensible and practical purposes, the only way to run the railway. Harvey knew it, too. When Harvey called him "Lieutenant" it was just anger talking. Harvey's anger was one they all felt and would feel forever. They all took the same risks, and they all felt the same frustration when the bad guys got away through the courts. Sometimes the good guys got away, too. "We're just the garbagemen, Harvey. We pick up the trash. Somebody else has to sort it out—we haven't got the time."

"And where it goes, nobody knows," Dana said. "Until it's too late, of course."

Stryker turned on her with a sudden anger of his own. "When did you know it was a woman?" he demanded.

Neilson answered for her. "She knew last night. At the hospital she said something about catching 'her.' I thought she was just tired but..."

"When we were chasing her, some of her hair escaped from under the cap," Dana explained. "But that wasn't it, really, because lots of men have long hair. It was her neck. With a long, slender neck like that, chances were it was a woman. And then I remembered what you said—about them both being police officers, and then divorcing after the boy was murdered. Well, if Rivera could seek revenge, why couldn't *Mrs*. Rivera seek it, too?"

"You never said anything—all night, when we were looking for Rivera, you never said a goddamn thing about it," Stryker said. "We might have picked her up last night."

"Oh, yeah—and Eberhardt might still be alive," Neilson said. "Isn't *that* a shame?"

"She should have said something," Stryker said stubbornly.

Dana nodded. "Yes, I should have. I'm sorry." She looked down at the puddle her dripping clothes had created. "I could have been wrong. You got everything else right—what did it matter if it was the husband or the wife? The theory was right either way. If we went after one, we'd miss the other—and vice versa. And I wasn't all *that* certain, anyway. I'd never seen Michael Rivera—he could have had a long, slender neck. I thought I'd just wait and see. If we'd found Rivera first, and it wasn't him, then he might have been able to tell us where she was. When I saw her in the graveyard, actually standing up, I could see right away she was much smaller than five ten. You said Michael Rivera was five ten. I knew it was his wife. So—I went after her."

"If you think back, we also told you Mike Rivera could disguise himself," Neilson said angrily. "He's quite capable of making himself look small. You could have been killed, dammit! If it had been Mike you were chasing, you could be dead, you damn fool! He's a judo black belt, for crying out loud! He carries a commando knife down the back of his damn neck! You could have been hurt, you could have been killed—" The thoughts were piling in on him, the horror of it clear in his face.

Dana looked at him and at Stryker. Both were
watching her. The enormity of the risk she had taken
suddenly caught up with her. She had tried to do their
job, tried to be a real cop—and she wasn't. She had
been lucky. Very, very lucky. They realised it—and
now she did, too.

She began to shake. She had been so certain it was
Carla, and she had been right, she had been *right*. But
she could have been wrong. She had been carried
away, wanting to impress them, wanting to impress
herself. And now the shaking was worse. She couldn't
stop shaking—

"Oh, Harvey—" She ran to him.

Startled, he put his arms around her, and patted her
rather awkwardly. Laugh this one off, Neilson, a voice
in his head said. Pretend this doesn't matter. Pretend
this one is tough and can't be hurt. But he couldn't,
because he knew it wasn't true. She was depending on
him for something—he hoped to God he could figure
out what it was and how to give it. "I'm sorry," he
mumbled. "I didn't mean to yell. You're all tired out,
aren't you? Poor kid—come on. I'll take you home.
I'll look after you. It's all right. Really. It's all right."

Stryker stared after them, and would have laughed
if he could have found the strength. Harvey Neilson?
Looking after someone else? Impossible. Absolutely
impossible.

Now they were getting into the car. Neilson was
backing off and taking her to her hotel without even
asking permission to leave the scene. Stryker started
forwards to remind Neilson that he was still on duty,
then paused. What the hell, he decided. Let it go.

Harvey had enough problems ahead of him without a petty hassle about duty.

And the job was done, wasn't it?

Someone tapped him on the shoulder. "Lieutenant Stryker?" It was one of the local precinct men. "I got a phone patch for you here—guy says it's urgent."

He managed to drag himself over to the patrol car and sank down, shivering, onto the seat. He picked up the receiver. "Stryker."

Pinsky's voice came out of the speaker. It was thin and desperate. "Jesus, Jack, you got to get over here to the hospital. It's Tos."

Stryker felt his heart turn over. "Is he worse?"

Pinsky's voice was frantic. "Hell, no—he's demanding his pants. He wants to go home, and they won't let him. He's threatening to call a lawyer. He's making an awful lot of noise—I haven't had a wink of sleep all night. You'd better get over here right away."

THIRTY

STRYKER WATCHED THE PLANE touch down, and again
flexed his arm cautiously. First day out of the sling,
and it felt very strange and vulnerable. As long as she
didn't expect him to carry her suitcases, he thought he
could get away with it until they went to bed and she
saw the bandage over the wound.

Last thing he wanted was a scene at the airport.

Around him swirled the same transitory life that had
been there just a week before. People saying hello,
people saying good-bye, people running to catch a
flight, people coming back laden with luggage. There
was a smell of onions and hamburger from a nearby
snack bar, and somewhere a child was crying. Flecked
through the crowds were the uniforms of the various
airlines, official and impressive against the bright colours of the travellers and tourists. Ticket machines,
teletypes, and typewriters clattered around him, and
there was the whisper and shuffle of a thousand footsteps.

Everybody was busy except himself.

The Narcotics Division was following up the "red
socks" scam, and were certain to make a big haul of
pushers and suppliers. "Brother" Feeney hadn't
talked yet. But he would, he would.

The Justice Department was closing in on the
Abiding Light Association, and cutting off its tenta-
cles one by one. There was talk of a Senate subcom-

mittee, indictments, scandal. The papers and television hadn't gotten a real hold on it yet. But they would, they would.

At the moment they were full of Carla Rivera.

The search for the cop killer was over.

Cops could cover the streets with one less thing to fear—but only one less. The city was still full of evil. He wished he felt more like taking it on. Maybe after a rest, he would. He might.

He felt very alone, standing there.

Tos was still in the hospital. Maybe they'd visit him on the way home. Where Stryker and the doctors had failed, his mother had succeeded. One good scolding from her and Tos had stopped arguing and done what he was told. There was a residual weakness in his left leg and arm that required physiotherapy. A week more in the hospital, then working out at home, would probably bring him back onto the strength in a month or two.

He said if they'd asked him he could have told them about Eberhardt and solved the whole thing, easy.

They'd told him to shut up and keep doing the exercises.

Pinsky was at home, bruised and battered and surrounded by wife, kids, dog (still doing tricks), and a fresh supply of books from the library. There was also a Sherlock Holmes series running on Channel 10. He was happy. He'd be back to work in a week.

Neilson? Neilson was on vacation. Bemused, protective, as cautiously gentle as a newly trained elephant with an egg, he was looking after Dana. She was letting him. They weren't thinking much beyond that.

And here I am, thought Stryker.

Someone named Kate is going to come off that plane. I haven't the least idea who she'll be—only that she'll be different than the Kate I waved good-bye to seven days ago.

It seemed to take a long time between the plane setting down and the moment when Kate emerged from Customs and flew into his arms. He tried not to grunt too loudly when she hugged him, and when they at last let go of one another, her eyes were shining.

"A man got on the plane in Boston with a newspaper. You caught the sniper!" She squeezed his arm— fortunately, the good one.

"Sure thing—all by myself, too! With my toy water pistol." He gazed at her in delight, undid the button on her jacket, then did it up again, before things got out of hand.

"All right, all right." She knew enough about him by now to realise her mistake. She straightened his tie. "I see the *team* has caught the killer," she said carefully.

"Not soon enough, but yes." He brushed her hair back from her temples.

"And it was a woman—really, a woman?" She stroked his ear.

"Afraid so." He kissed her chin.

"Was she insane?" She smoothed his cheek.

"Afraid so." He grinned down at her. They were both so glad to see one another that nothing else seemed to have any real substance.

"It's not funny," she reproached him.

He nodded and sighed. "You're telling me."

They went to retrieve her luggage and, fortunately, found a trolley to put it on. As he reached for the larger case, she stepped ahead of him. "Better let me do that, you might start your shoulder bleeding," she said, hefting it off the carousel and onto the trolley.

He stood there, staring at her, while her smaller case went off on another circuit of the carousel. "My shoulder?" he said idiotically.

She grinned and watched her small case disappear around the curve. "After I talked to you, I called Nell Pinsky, of course. She told me everything that was in the papers and on television, about Tos, about you, everything."

"Is that why you didn't call again? Why you haven't called for the past two days?"

She nodded, then leaned down and snatched the case from the carousel before it got away again. "You said you could handle it, so I let you handle it."

"Kate . . ."

She dropped the case onto the trolley and looked at him. "No, it wasn't easy, and yes, I hated doing it, and yes, I still hate what you do. But I had to see if I *could* do it, if I could stand not knowing. If I could trust you not to get yourself . . ." She couldn't actually say it. She didn't have to. Her eyes said it all. "I love you. I'm supposed to be intelligent, but that doesn't seem to apply to loving you. I haven't been doing it very well. However, I do know that if I tried to change one thing I might change everything and then you wouldn't be you, would you?" Her eyes were filled with tears. He put his good arm around her and drew her close. "And anyway," she said, her voice muffled into his shoulder, "I thought a lot while I was away. I realised I could get along without you very well—but I didn't want to do it. I had a long talk with Nell—just wait

until you see the phone bill—and she's going to give
me lessons about being a police wife. Okay?''

Better Nell than Carla Rivera, Stryker thought, but
he didn't say it. All he said, softly and gratefully, was
"Okay."

As they walked along, pushing the trolley ahead of
them for all the world like a strolling couple pushing
a baby buggy, he told her about the case. It was easier
than trying to find the words about loving her that always seemed to start out well and come out stupid. He
could *show* her that he loved her, but she deserved
more. She walked beside him, her hair gleaming in the
sun, the curls tossed by the wind, her mouth soft, her
eyes wide and a little pink, still, with tears. He decided to try and read more poetry.

"Okay," Kate said. "Start at the beginning."

Stryker made a face. "It starts with cops being human and making mistakes. None of them so terrible
in themselves, but all to do with the same person, and
all adding up to a chain of trouble." He gave her the
background on the victims.

"And when Eberhardt finally killed, as he probably would have even if none of those mistakes had
been made, he happened to pick the son of a cop—
David Rivera."

"It must have been terrible for them. The last thing
they would have expected."

"It was terrible. The most terrible thing about it was
that we couldn't get him convicted for it. Maybe that
was the worst mistake—and it was mine. Mine and
Tos's."

"You did your best."

"Yes, we did. Better than our best—but it wasn't good enough. Not for Carla, anyway. When Eberhardt murdered her son, Carla Rivera didn't take it like Mike. He had faith, he accepted what he saw as God's decision. It humbled him, made him want to be a better person. But she was angry. Her bitterness was directed as much at the department as at the killer. She knew what an ideal cop would be—she'd nearly been one herself. She'd won citations for bravery and initiative, she had trophies for marksmanship same as Mike did, downtown had an eye on her right from the academy. She knew how it all *should* be done. She knew opportunities to stop Eberhardt must have occurred again and again, and had gone by. As her bitterness grew, her judgement wasted away. She became obsessive about 'good cops' and 'bad cops,' and she decided that any men who had let Eberhardt continue on the road that led to her son's death were as much to blame as he was. She went to a department psychiatrist before she resigned, but it didn't do much good. In her eyes, those men had killed her son. It was all she could think about. She left Mike, and then there was no balancing factor to keep her steady. As time went by, her rage took over. Eventually there was nothing left of Carla Rivera *but* rage—and the ability to apply it."

"But how did she find out about all of them? And why didn't you find out sooner?"

Stryker looked bleak. It was a question they had asked themselves again and again. "In a working week, your average cop may have occasion to face dozens of situations, not all of them criminal by the book. If they are clearly criminal, he has to go by the book or the DA can't make a case. A lot of situations are borderline, maybe not criminal at all—like domestic arguments, for instance—and the cop on the scene does the best he can to use his common sense to settle them there and then. So a lot of situations never result in arrests. Even so, he *will* arrest a lot of offenders, ranging from traffic offenses right up to homicide. Over a working life, his arrests can number thousands. And we were looking at the working lives of seven cops, Kate, some short—like Santosa's, and some long, like mine. Each time an incident occurs, we have to make a report, and all the reports and so on go into the files. Now, the thing about computers is that they do *exactly* what you tell them to do. We told it to look at *arrests*. We *didn't* tell it to look at the ones who got away, because we figured the ones who got away would carry no grudge, right?''

"I guess not," Kate allowed.

"There were thousands, literally thousands, and we were in the process of checking them all out. Each new death brought a whole new set to follow up. We were also looking for arrests that all of the victims had in common, which slowed things up even more, because not all of us arrested the little bastard. Plus which, all the time, we were looking at it ass backwards. If you knew what to look for, and at, it *was* all there in the computer. If you looked at *Eberhardt's* record, including all the reports that related to him, whether they resulted in an *arrest* or not, you would find the names of all the cops involved in his life. Carla Rivera started out with Eberhardt—we started out with the cops who were killed. We were looking for what

they had in common, and not what someone else—
Eberhardt—had in common with them. You see?''

"Yes, I see. And Carla Rivera did that?''

"When her boy was killed they thought it would be
better if she came off the street for a while," Stryker
said. "They assigned her to Records.''

"Oh Lord.''

"Yeah. Apparently she was real good in Records.
Used to work overtime. They were sorry when she left
the department, they said.''

"Where is she, now?''

"In a hospital, with a lot of psychiatrists talking to
her. From what I hear, she's not doing any talking
back. They say that in her eyes she's perfectly well
adjusted. She has accomplished what she set out to do.
What happens now is irrelevant to her.''

"That poor woman.''

He glanced at her. "That 'poor woman' nearly
killed me, babe, remember? And *did* kill six people,
including Eberhardt. Don't you have any hate in
you?''

"No,'' Kate said.

"Good,'' he said. "Hate is where it all goes wrong
for a cop. Or a cop's wife.''

They had reached the car. "You know the worst
part?'' he asked reflectively. "It was when Mike Rivera arrived at the precinct where we were holding his
ex-wife. Mike stood there, shaking his head and crying and asking her 'Why?', and Carla stared right
through him, as if Mike were not there at all. As if he
didn't exist, maybe as if he'd never existed. And yet
David had been his child, too. That got me, Kate. That
was bad.''

She reached out and took his hand. After a moment he came back from wherever he'd gone and smiled at her. "The crazy thing is, it was something Rivera himself said that finally put us on the right track."

"Really?"

"Yeah. He told Ned Pinsky that it's the things we *don't* do that are often the most important."

Kate looked sideways at him, then looked around for a litter bin. From the depths of her big flight bag, she dug out a new-looking book, entitled, *Seductive Semantics*. On the back, a photo of Richard Cotterell, handsome and brooding, stared out. She dumped the book into the bin and came back to her impossible policeman.

"He's *so* right," she said.

A SENSITIVE CASE
ERIC WRIGHT

AN INSPECTOR CHARLIE SALTER MYSTERY

THE BIGGER THEY ARE THE HARDER THEY FALL

The murder of masseuse Linda Thomas was a sticky situation—her clients included big people in high places. It was a case for Special Affairs Inspector Charlie Salter and his chief investigator, Sergeant Mel Pickett. They delicately kick open a hornet's nest of hostile, secretive suspects, including a provincial deputy minister, a famous television host, the tenants of the woman's building, a nervous academic, a secret lover and an unidentified man—the last person to see Linda alive.

A lot of people had a lot to hide—and even more at stake than their careers. To make things more difficult, Salter is worried his wife is having an affair.

It's a sensitive case, both at home and on the job. Charlie's doing a lot of tiptoeing around—with a killer lurking in the shadow of every step.

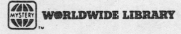

HAL'S OWN MURDER CASE
LEE MARTIN

LABOR PAINS

Two weeks away from the birth of her baby, Ft. Worth detective
Deb Ralston decided her sixteen-year-old son, Hal, had picked a rotten
time to hitchhike halfway across the state with his girlfriend, Lorie, and be
arrested for murder.

The victim, a young woman, had been hacked with Hal's hunting knife
and left in Lorie's sleeping bag. Now Lorie is missing and Hal's in jail.

Ralston hits the tiny East Texas town in her official capacity as worried
mother—a role that quickly expands into investigating officer. The trail
leads to places of the heart no mother-to-be wants to go...but with a cop's
unerring instinct, she follows the ugly path into the twisted mind of a
ruthless killer.

Flight to
YESTERDAY
VELDA JOHNSTON

A NIGHTMARE REVISITED

Dubbed a "young Jean Harris" by the press, Sara Hargreaves
spent four years in prison for a crime of passion she didn't
commit. Now she's escaped, and she's desperate to clear her
name and to see her dying mother.

As her face appears nightly on the local news, Sara disguises
herself, and with the help of a young law student she is forced to
trust, she returns to the scene of the crime.

The fashionable sanatorium where handsome plastic surgeon
Dr. Manuelo Covarrubias was stabbed with a knife bearing Sara's
fingerprints looks much the same. But as Sara begins her flight
to yesterday, the secrets surrounding the callous playboy doctor
who jilted her unfold. Secrets that once drove someone to
murder...secrets that could kill again.

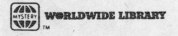

HUGH PENTECOST
WITH INTENT TO KILL

MURDER CHECKS IN...

Murder is an unwelcome spotlight on Pierre Chambrun's beloved hotel. All the more unwelcome when the mutilated body is that of a fifteen-year-old boy and when the mystery further involves a pop idol, a brutally beaten centerfold, a soft-porn king, a religious zealot, an employee found dead in a laundry hamper and another with a concussion.

It's a convoluted case worthy of the dapper Chambrun. But time is running out as the murderer readies to strike again.

"Suspenseful with a surprise ending."

— *Clarion Ledger/Daily News*

 **WORLDWIDE LIBRARY**